BORN TO BE
Colored
Together

Born to be Colored Together

Not Your Ordinary Love Story

Manly E. Hogg

Born to be Colored Together

Copyright © 2019 by Manly E. Hogg. All rights reserved.

No part of this publication may be reproduced, stored in a retrieval system or transmitted in any way by any means, electronic, mechanical, photocopy, recording or otherwise without the prior permission of the author except as provided by USA copyright law.

This novel is a work of fiction. Names, descriptions, entities, and incidents included in the story are products of the author's imagination. Any resemblance to actual persons, events, and entities is entirely coincidental.

The opinions expressed by the author are not necessarily those of URLink Print and Media.

1603 Capitol Ave., Suite 310 Cheyenne, Wyoming USA 82001
1-888-980-6523 | admin@urlinkpublishing.com

URLink Print and Media is committed to excellence in the publishing industry.

Book design copyright © 2018 by URLink Print and Media. All rights reserved.

Published in the United States of America
ISBN 978-1-64367-322-6 (Paperback)
ISBN 978-1-64367-321-9 (Digital)

Fiction
21.03.19

CHAPTER 1

Coming of Age

The sun was setting over the horizon as it always has so many millenniums ago, but today was different... today two souls were watching with amazement at an eagle gracefully circling high above a snowcapped mountain's peak.

Dawn Whitecloud and her father, a Cheyenne Chief known as Red Moon, was in deep discussion about Dawn's future in the world of "*The White man,*" as her father would so coldly put it.

"Dawn, today is your forthright day, the day of your womanhood," he said with a solemn voice, as his heart was heavy at the thought of lending his only daughter to the outside world even if it was to further her education.

Chief Red Moon and his ancestors were of a different time, a different world. If his people were to move ahead, even he would have to let go of a little tradition, although it pained him terribly to do so. He saw much potential in Dawn from an early age, always inquisitive, always resourceful even in matters reserved for only that of The Tribal Council elders. She had a light in her eyes, which illuminated so brightly, that not even The Great Spirit could deny her slightest whim. Full of life and love was she, always graceful and always most respectful. Red Moon had always hoped to keep his precious daughter by his side to help on his modest ranch on the Pine Ridge Indian Reservation he struggled yearly to turn a profit with. Yet how could he deny nurturing such potential?

Dawn could be of any profession she chooses. I must let her go now, to pursue whatever it is she dreams of as her sweet brown eyes travel to the Dream World every night and even sometimes during the day, as he would seldom catch her staring off into oblivion. Her hands would take on a mind of their own as they continued doing her chores despite the severed consciousness. He was always amazed at how she could manage such a feat. *She is well prepared this day to venture forth into a new era for herself and our people. This to Ma'heo'o, The Creator, I pray.*

This moment seemed to come much too fast for Red Moon. It seemed as if he had just celebrated her sweet 16th birthday. Even then she had looked to be a full-grown woman. In the ancient days she would have mated at that time with a young warrior. He would have gracefully handed over many horses and much land, for the hand of a Chief's daughter was an ultimate prize, especially with an Indian maiden as beautiful as Dawn. That was then and much has changed.

Had two winters come and gone so fast since Dawns Vision Quest? Red Moon turned to his daughter and looked deep into her dark brown eyes.

"You must decide on a future so I can prepare the Spirits for your coming with prayer."

Dawn looked at her father with a puzzled frown. "Father, I don't understand."

Red Moon turned and pointed at the magnificent American Bald Eagle as it navigated the heavens, daring for even the smallest of movement below.

"That eagle you see in superior flight is just another bird to most, but to our people it will hear your words and carry them to the Maiyun, the spirits, as swift as the lightening can strike. You need but to whisper and its keen ears will hear all. Dawn, you are the daughter of a Cheyenne Chief and in my day, a squaws…ah," Red Moon cleared his throat and continued, "a woman's place was with the man that proved his loyalty to the tribe. He would have a Warriors Bonnet full of War Feathers from many a battle with rival tribes. Dawn we live in a new time and if our people, our custom and our beliefs are to survive, we must move with the wind or die out as with the Buffalo."

Dawn gazed suspiciously at the eagle, which was now on a swift dive in prey of some unfortunate creature below. She pondered how such a creature could have such cognitive and spiritual powers, but she has come to accept her parent's beliefs as her own and decides to abide by her father's notions.

"I want to help our people father," said Dawn with conviction.

"I would like to take the scholarship to USC and from there I hope to major in Law."

Red moon responded surprisingly, "Our people could use much legal advice in the coming years, but I always thought you would pursue a career in medicine."

"Medicine!" Dawn looked at her father in shock. She reminisce back when she was growing up how her parents spun tales of great Medicine Men with super natural powers. Even now, she could see the medicine pouch around her father's neck, which no doubtlessly held Parts from dead animals and herbs from Mother Earth.

"Pejuta Wicasa, our tribal shaman were only second to the chief of the tribe," explained Red Moon, "Medicine men were the chiefs' right hand man as the Americans says."

Dawn giggled with pride in her father not saying "*The White Man or Pale Faces*," as he used to while she was growing up on the reservation. "Your grandfather was a very wise Shaman in his cycle of moons.

He helped our people on many occasions with his visions. He is on the Ghost Trail journey as we speak as his road on this mortal plain has come to a close. It will not be long before *White Buffalo* passes on to the spirit world. His medicine was of great power but it was of an old time when our people needed more guidance than healing. You, my precious one, are of this time and I have had a vision of you performing great miracles of healing the bodies as well as the minds of others."

"I understand this Father, but do you think I would be taken seriously as a doctor with the Sioux and the Cheyenne of our reservation?" asked Dawn with skepticism.

Red Moon thought deeply of his daughter's words and he felt her concern for her treatment among the Sioux to be a truly insightful concern indeed. He knew without a doubt that no Cheyenne would test his patience where his precious daughter was concerned, but the Teton Sioux was another thing. The Lakota were just as traditional in preserving the ancient ways, as were the Northern Cheyenne, sometimes even more so. *It's a wonder we survived at all in this new age among the Americans.*

Red Moon put his strong right hand on Dawns shoulder to comfort her, but mainly to pause and allow thoughts to reel through his mind as he awaited guidance from the spirits. He used his left hand to place her long raven black hair off her right shoulder and let it flow to her back and into the breeze as if to make sure her ears were unobstructed to his next words for he was sure they would change her life-line forever. He went on to ponder... *Dawn speaks strongly of helping our people, but I'm afraid her heart will not be strong enough to battle in the courts of the corporate world for lands and artifacts promised returned to us. Corporate Lawyers are too ruthless as they are paid much to be so. Government representatives are no better. You would think they had personal rights to the land and our ancient treasures the way they bargain for them so. No, a lawyer's life would taint her spirit. This I am sure of as my heart and mind whisper to me. Dawn has always showed a kindness towards even that of the smallest of animals most would otherwise consider dinner. Medicine would be a nobler path for her spirit, but it will be ultimately up to her and the Great Spirit to decide. I will leave it in the hands of Ma'heo'o. All I can do as a father is to reassure her and blanket her from her fears of acceptance among our people, for it would be a blessing to have her return to us, after many circles of seasons has passed during her learning.*

"My child, a little more than century ago the Sioux of Dakota and the Cheyenne of Wyoming were bitter rivals. They were equal in strength and courage. They battled on this very ground for prime hunting land during the beginning of the Laramie treaty when no tribe understood the true meaning of its words.

Thanks to the union of your great-grandfather, *War Hawk*, a Cheyenne Chief, to your great-grandmother, *Fox with Blue Tail*, a Sioux Chiefs' only daughter, we today share a common bond on this reservation that has stood the test of time. Nothing is impossible, my sweet daughter and as long as you are the daughter of Chief Red Moon you *will* have the respect of every Soul on this reservation." Red Moon looked deep into Dawns' Ebony brown eyes and stated, "That I can promise you."

Dawn in return, looked deep into her fathers' eyes. His eyes always showed his conviction of the words he told her. His features, very strong and typical of his full blooded Cheyenne heritage. When his dark brown eyes had a glistening reddish look to them she knew that he felt deeply about his words. Today he was definitely serious. Today she would take his every word to heart.

"Father, I will pursue medicine as a career!"

"I'm proud of your decision darling," expressed Red Moon with much joy. Red Moon turned to face the Eagle making off with its prey deeply clawed. He bellowed at the top of his voice in the native Algonquian tongue of the Cheyenne, "Tell the Spirits to listen to our prayers closely tonight for Dawn Whitecloud, Daughter of Chief Red Moon, is to venture out into the world of the Americans and become a great Warrior of Medicine!"

Dawn could only smile with happiness to make her father so proud of her. She would apply for college soon and major in medicine. She would do this for her people, but mainly for her father who always expressed his concern for her future and his heartfelt pride for her.

Dawn gripped her father's hand tightly as they headed back down the steep slope and into the forest of Ponderosa Pines, which led to the riverbed below. Red Moon stooped down various times along the way to pick special herbs. Only a selected few knew of these potent herbs and the powers one could derive from them. Apart, they would have no true effects, but blended together, it's said that it could make a man feel as one with Nature herself. Tonight Red

Moon's *special blend* will be smoked in his most cherished Pipe as he prayed to the Spirits. He and all the other Elders on the reservation will sit around a great fire and pray to the Spirits to watch over Dawn and give her guidance on her long journey amongst the Americans. Her mother, Fawn Running Deer, will make a great feast and after all has eaten; her younger brother, Black Wolf, would lead the other young Warriors in a *Dance of Celebration* to consecrate Dawns' 18th birthday. Today she has become a Woman.

CHAPTER 2

First Day

Dawn enTereD The brightly-lit halls of USC. With every step of her moccasin-adorned feet, she could feel her heart throbbing strongly with nervous anticipation. Today was the biggest day of her life. She will use the tuition from the American Indian College Fund to purchase her dream of being a Physician. She couldn't help but wonder how many Native Americans walked these very halls before her in pursuit of the very same dreams.

As Dawn approached the school auditorium she could see the long line of potential USC graduates.

"Attention please, attention all enrollees," loudly bellowed a raspy voiced woman over the intercom. Startled, Dawn stopped to listen.

"Please form a single line in front of the course you will be enrolling during the first semester, Thank you."

Dawn moved ahead to the line for Biology 301. Standing in front of her was a faddishly dressed woman. She couldn't help but notice the tremendous length of her hair.

"Ahem!" Dawn cleared her throat to attract the young female. "Excuse me please … miss," she said quietly.

Katwana Delores Jones or KD as her friends called her, an African American, was slightly overweight for her height but knew how to wear her clothing well enough to hide that fact. She quickly turned around, as if to say, *"why are you in my world cause I damn sure as hell didn't invite you!"* She immediately started looking Dawn up and down. Dawn never experienced this type of posturing before and was quite shocked into silence. KD looked into Dawns deep brown eyes and saw innocence that she never thought possible in any human being just before Dawn's head lowered to the floor. She placed her finger on Dawns' chin and solemnly raised Dawns head to look into her eyes again.

"You have beautiful hair," Dawn thought to mention to break the ice.

"It must have taken you years to grow it so long and thick." KD couldn't help but chuckle at her naive remark.

"Girl, you are a piece of work!"

"My name is Katwana, but my friends call me KD."

"Nice to meet you KD. My name is Dawn." A relief came over her suddenly as she gazed upon the gold toothed smile of this person that just a second ago seemed to want to eat her alive like some starving beast of the wild.

KD took a step back, "Dawn what in the world do you have on your puppy dogs girlfriend?" Dawn looked down at what she must have been describing.

"My puppy… oh my feet," she replied with embarrassment. "Oh, they are called moccasins," she explained.

"My tribe, the Cheyenne, actually still make them by hand." "Well that's just find I guess if you are a tourist but if you're hangin with me girlfriend, then we have to get you with the times, baby girl."

All Dawn could do was smile at KD because she knew that she just connected with a kindred spirit. She thought of the saying, you can't judge a book by its cover and that sure fitted her new friend KD. She just hoped she wouldn't look too silly with a gold tooth and nose earring as KD wore so well.

With courses enrolled and tuition's paid, Dawn and KD walked back to the school's female dormitory.

"What room you in girlfriend?" KD asked using the Ebonics language even though she was very fluent with the Queens English.

"I'm in 2D," replied Dawn curiously.

"Not for long baby girl," said KD as she changed the names on the room assignment board to reflect Dawn as her roommate. "I didn't want no snobby gray girl for no roommate anyhow."

Dawn was puzzled at KD's remark but knew enough about her already to be smart enough to leave that one alone. Although she still pondered how a person's skin could be **Gray** as she followed KD back to their room to unpack.

Dawn was neatly folding her clothes when she had noticed KD holding a small picture frame tightly to her bosom. She thought nothing of it till she noticed tears in KD's eyes. Dawn thought to let her have a moment to herself so she graciously started walking out of the room.

"Hey, where are you headed, young lady?" asked KD.

"Oh, I was ah . . ." Dawn was at a loss of a good excuse and KD saw right through her, but appreciated the gesture.

"Come back here, you. Don't mind me. I'm just trippin a little," demanded KD.

KD motioned Dawn over to her side of the room. Dawn looked at the photo inside the gold rimmed picture frame. She smiled at the cute little boy that was missing his front teeth in the photo.

"Ah, he's so adorable, KD. Is he your little brother?" asked Dawn thinking the boy looked too old to be anything else but a younger brother or nephew.

"No, he's my son. At least he **was** my son," replied KD sorrowfully.

"Is he okay? You seem so sad," asked Dawn feeling KD's pain.

"I haven't talked about this with anyone since it happened, but I was so young and naive back then. All I could think about was keeping it a secret so I could move on with my life as if it never happened."

"What never happened, KD, I don't understand?"

"I had Jose' when I was only 14. My parents never even knew I was pregnant because I was always a full figured gal. I don't know,

I guess I was hoping that it would just go away or I would miscarry. God, I even thought to stick a wire . . ." KD burst out with an uncontrollable cry. Dawn sat down beside her and put her arms around her for comfort.

"I don't know what I was thinking, Dawn. My mom didn't take it too well when she found out. I was planning on keeping it from her as well, but my water broke while I was in class. I've never been so humiliated before in my life."

Dawn wiped a tear from KD's eye as the two chuckled to keep from crying.

"So where's your little boy?" asked Dawn excited to meet him someday.

"That's what I was crying about. My mother and I had decided it best to put the baby up for adoption. You think I would have given my baby boy a Spanish name? I would have called him Julius Jamal Jones, JJ for short."

KD smiled at the picture and showed Dawn where she had written JJ on the back of the frame. Dawn was curious to one other fact though. KD never mentioned about what her father must have thought about the situation. She was brought up to believe that the father always had a say-so in matters such as this. But she thought to leave that question for another day.

CHAPTER 3

The Game

Dawn and KD sat at the 50-yard line first row benches at USC stadium. It was dawn's first Football game she had ever attended in person. She remembered catching the Super Bowls on T.V growing up on the reservation. But today she realized that it definitely was not the same as being here in person even though it was only a college game. The sheer excitement of everyone around her heightened her new experience and she felt part of a much bigger tribe called the USC Trojans.

It was the 4th quarter and the Trojans were down by 5 points. The time was wounding down but there was just enough time for a long throw from the 45-yard mark.

"Trevor, man you got to lay it on me around the 15, bro!" yelled Darryl over the heckling of the UCLA Bruins alumni.

"Yeah right Mon-G, you are, oh let's see ... 2 for 5 this game!" said the quarterback Trevor (The Ju) Tregoning.

"Face it my man, you've put your body to the limit this season and it's definitely showing this game and I for one would like to see the Rose Bowl this year." The rest of the team in the huddle couldn't help but agree with Trevor.

Darryl Jackson, a.k.a. Mon-G as his team had nicknamed him, was one of the finest receivers in college football. He lost his focus this game due to the pain in his right knee. It wasn't enough to inhibit his game but he didn't want to chance a serious injury that would keep him out of the limelight. He had people he loved that were counting on him to make it to the NFL.

Darryl spun out of the huddle in anger. As he looked over the stadium of fans he couldn't help but notice this perfect face that seemed to calm him in an instant. It was Dawn and she connected with his eyes as she noticed him looking in her direction with a curious expression on his handsome face. She couldn't help but smile as she turned to KD and caught her giving her a look as if to say, *"Girl, you just attracted one of the most popular men in school, now what are you going to do about it?"*

Dawn giggled and hit KD on the shoulder for even thinking such a thing, especially after she had already told her of the planned union with an Indian Warrior from her home. KD was shocked at how Dawn was able to read her mind.

Darryl swung back in the huddle with a new focus and exclaimed, "I **will** be open at the 15!"

"Okay Mon-G my man, but if you're not, I'm going long into the in zone. It's 3rd down and we need more than a field goal to tie so we might as well go for the win or nothing... Break!" The team clapped in unison and lined up on their 45-yard line.

Darryl loosened his leg up as the quarterback called the snap. He was willing to change for this newfound woman of his dreams what he would have only chanced for an NFL scout. He didn't know if it would be worth it but it was too late to sweat it now. The Ball snapped and on cue he broke ground as if his life depended on it. He was oblivious to the pain as he broke left off his right leg at the 22 and angled in towards the middle of the 15th. He looked back and Eagle-eyed a perfect spiral heading towards him slightly above his head. A quick jump at the precise moment put the leather square in the palm of his hands. As his feet touched down he went into high gear and sprinted to the goal line with the ease of his namesake, Mon-G that was short for Mongoose in Hip-Hop lingo.

The umpires threw their hands up to signify a touchdown, the whistles blew and the crowd roared with excitement at one of the year's best games that will ultimately put them in running for the Rose Bowl Championships.

After Darryl cabbage patched his victory in the in zone he managed to work himself free from the accolades the team and cheerleaders laid on him and walked back to where Dawn was sitting to present her with the winning ball.

"I want you to have this," said Darryl.

"But you don't even know me," said Dawn shyly. "My name is Darryl and I'm a senior."

"Hi, I'm Dawn and my friend is Katwana."

"Nice to meet you Katwana and . . ." Darryl paused at an interruption from KD.

"You can call me KD," she said trying to be noticed as well.

"It's nice to meet you KD and very nice to meet **you**, Dawn." Dawn couldn't help but smile at Darryl's charm.

"Thanks to you, I found my motivation to make that play so you deserve this," he said as he handed Dawn the ball.

As Dawn took the ball she looked at KD and then at Darryl and she knew at that moment that the Spirits were testing her and she had hopelessly failed them. Her life at that moment would change forever because she had just connected with a forbidden thing. It would be bad enough to her family that Darryl was American but an African American, she thought may accumulate a whole different set of problems.

Darryl gave Dawn a big set of pearly whites. "See you around precious," he said as he sped off to his adoring fans and teammates.

KD interlocked her arm around Dawns and led her back to the dorm as Dawn gazed at the game ball with mixed emotions.

"Don't let it scare you Dawn," KD said sensing Dawns' perturb demeanor.

"You're a very pretty girl with all that fine long black hair. Come on Dawn, you knew that eventually some fine young stud was bound to recognize it and be on your case. Ain't no Indians around here girlfriend unless they're from the Middle East or something. Trust me," KD went on to say, "You could do a lot worst, baby girl. I know, look at the men I've been stuck with lately."

They both had to laugh at that one and it brought Dawn comfort to know that KD was there for her and understood her concerns for a relationship with an African American. KD knew exactly what Dawn needed at the moment.

"You got a man?" asked KD with a song like tone.

"I already got a man!" replied Dawn as she remembered the song KD played for her one day that tickled her so much.

Dawn and KD sang aloud in unison as they skipped back to the dorm, "What that man got to do with me! I already got a man! I'm not trying to hear that you see!"

CHAPTER 4

First love

There was a knock at the door that startled Dawn as she was deep into her studies. Biology had never been her favorite subject, but her teachers always told her she had a knack for it. At least she did once she got over the initial shock of seeing the poor animals floating in jars of alcohol or pinned sadistically to a wooden board as its insides spewed out all gray and slimy.

"The doors open," she said as she turned to see who was about to disturb her, which may possibly keep her from acing her next exam.

Dawn couldn't help but swell with anxiety as Darryl swung open the door and entered her dorm room. A Sensuous smile developed on Dawns face as her eyes met Darryl's deep browns. Darryl had planned what he would say at this moment earlier but now he couldn't seem to find the words. All he could do was stand there and smile at Dawn's Loveliness. She was definitely the most gorgeous woman he has ever had the privilege of knowing. He thought of her uniqueness and how wonderfully she carried her beauty.

"Well, are you coming in or just going to stand there looking handsome?" Dawn asked as she thought to herself what KD would say in this situation.

Darryl turned around and closed the door behind him as Dawn couldn't help but to stare at how well his jeans fitted around his tight gluteus maximums as KD so elegantly phrased it.

"I hope you didn't come here to get your ball back."

"No, I want you to keep it. You inspired that play more than you will ever know."

Dawn blushed to know that she was such an influence in such an important game. She came to realize later that night that their win against UCLA put her new school in the Championship Rose Ball Game. She still didn't quite grasp the significance of it all until KD added *Girl it's like the Super Bowl of College football, duh.*

"I want you to be at every game from now on as my personal cheer leader," demanded Darryl with a debonair smile.

"Wouldn't that make your girlfriend jealous?" asked Dawn fishing for a little info as to his romantic status.

"That would be a problem only if I had one," Darryl replied shyly as he looked down at his new Jordan's. Hiding his expression was Darryl's main objective as he pondered. *How am I going to explain such a relationship? Hell, I barely understand it myself. I have to be honest with Dawn. A woman like her deserves no less.*

"I find it hard to believe that such an eligible bachelor as yourself would be without a playmate for more than a second. So whom was the unlucky girl that just got her heart broken before you decided to grace me with your presence?"

"You have it all wrong Dawn," said Darryl with a defensive posture. *Man, she has some kind of sixth sense. Yeah, honesty is definitely the right move with Dawn.*

"I guess I'm still somewhat keeping in touch with my High School sweetheart."

"What do you mean by... somewhat in touch?" Dawn inquired disheartenly.

"Well, I guess she keeps in touched more than I do," he replied as he sat down at the foot of the bed the Football laid on.

"You see Dawn, I come from a pretty poor family from South Central, LA. I'm one of the very few from my High School that received a Football scholarship to USC or anywhere for that matter.

Everyone is counting on me to make it to the NFL or something. You know, put them on easy street. Unfortunately, my High School sweetheart is holding on to that very same dream even though there is no real love between us anymore. Come to think of it I never cared for her attitude much anyway. She was the head cheerleader and all. You know Miss Popular and all. I never felt real love for her. Everyone expected me to date the best and believe it or not even with her funky attitude she was considered the finest girl in the school. I guess I fell into that peer pressure trap."

"I see," sympathized Dawn.

"That kind of sounds like the same situation I'm in. My parents are poor too and I am also their only hope," continued Dawn solemnly, "I too have someone that I am to belong as my father has traditionally set in motion."

"You mean your people still do that in this day and age?" "Unfortunately, yes, at least it's that way for me, as my father is the chief of our tribe on the reserve. It is traditional for his daughter to join with a Warrior that has proven himself to our people. The one I am to join to is such a warrior. He is our greatest warrior and none will challenge him. For me to refuse to join to him would bring dishonor among my family and his band. I could not bear to dishonor my father and know such shame in my heart." Dawn replied as her head slumped from the thought. *Now you come into my Life-circle and I feel like there is hope for me. Have the Spirits sent you to me, my Darryl, to rescue me from a life of unhappiness? I must not give in to these ravenousness feelings deep within my heart for the price to pay may be too high. Yet how can I deny them? It seems so clear to me as if I've seen it before in a vision quest, but couldn't decipher its mysterious meaning. I am far from home in this New World and cannot seek the guidance of mother. What do the spirits want of me? No, What do I want for myself?*

Darryl reached out his hand to Dawn as she placed her hand in his. He pulled her towards him as she sat on the bed. They looked into each other's eyes... a deep long stares that pierced into the depth of the other's soul. They both knew at that very moment that there was a force beyond their understanding that brought them together. A force that would be virtually impossible to destroy.

Dawn allowed herself to collapse on Darryl's hard body, her lips now as one with his. Lost in the moment, they both became oblivious of the fact that they both belonged to another, another person, another people, another culture, another time, another religion, and another world.

Darryl began to caress the back of Dawn's thin neck with one hand while he cradled the other into the crevice of her back. He pulled her into him as she moaned with hurried anticipation. Dawn never felt this way before and she quite enjoyed being in Darryl's strong chiseled arms. Darryl rolled Dawn over as he raised up on his knees and removed his shirt with one swift motion. Dawn reached out; her eyes still shut, located Darryl's pecks and began to message him as hard as she could. Darryl returned the favor but he caressed her supple breast as gently as he dared. Dawn's now erect nipples was like the pleasure center of her body as Darryl used his tongue to seduce them into a hardened state which aroused her to a point close to ecstasy. All Dawn could do was to give in and let the moment continue as she whispered to Darryl, "Take me, my sweet lover."

Darryl smiled as he carried out Dawn's command as if he were a well-disciplined Marine. His now erect prowess was ready to carry out its first command. Darryl brought his warm damp hands to Dawn's shoulders as he placed his probing tongue to dawns navel. Dawn's pleasure center seemed to switch in an instant as Darryl began to slither his tongue from Dawns navel down to her now pulsating womanhood. Dawn found herself undoing Darryl's trousers and pulling them down to his knees as he gently pulled off her laced panties.

Darryl kicked off his trousers and just paused there on bent knee looking at Dawn in all her loveliness. He knew at that moment he had found his soul mate and at that exact moment the way Dawn was feeling she knew without a doubt that she had found something very special and very permanent as well.

Dawn found herself pulling Darryl into her after the anticipation of him entering her became too great to control any longer. Darryl was so erect at this point his strong manhood slid into Dawn's readily waiting womanhood with ease as she was already dripping wet from his belly button seductions.

"Hmmm, Oh Darryl!" exclaimed Dawn as he gently stroked her excited breast in unison with every rhythmic thrust of his manhood.

Darryl's motions started gentle as he could feel the tightness of Dawn's love chasm telling the tale of a young woman never before touch in this manner. This intensified his experience with Dawn tenfold. Darryl felt his thick swollen manhood sliding more freely and began to hasten his motions as Dawn palmed his buttocks pulling him into her deeper and deeper.

"Oh, Dawn!" Darryl moaned out uncontrollably as he exploded his juices deep inside her pulsating womb.

Exhausted, Darryl rolled over as Dawn suddenly found herself on top of him in one smooth motion. She was amazed at how he was able to do that and still keep himself deep inside her. Dawn grabbed the base of her hair and flung it over her head onto Darryl's heaving chest. As she straddled him she continued to flood in pools of ecstasy.

Darryl laid his left hand gently on Dawn's inner thigh and death gripped the ball he gave her with his right hand as his manhood continued to pulsate with every motion of Dawn's rotating hips. Finally, Dawn collapsed onto Darryl as she experienced an ultimate sense of immeasurable pleasure from deep within her womb. Dawn couldn't help but cry from happiness as she kissed Darryl's sweat drenched lips. There they lay, entwined as one, in a moment they wished could last forever as to not have to ever deal with the consequences that may come. But for now all they could do is to drift off into a deep satisfying sleep.

Morning had come and gone as Dawn and Darryl continued to enjoy their moment of togetherness. They were relieved to know that KD would be gone until Sunday evening as she had always returned at that time from being home for the weekend.

They would repeat last night as many time as their young bodies possibly would allow, only stopping briefly to nourish themselves. Such things were forbidden in the old days, but the old days to them at the moment was just that. Ancient ways to be long forgotten dust collected symbols, meaningless virtues in a world that has advanced past such ideological idiocies. At least that's the excuse their raging hormones allowed them to entertain.

The days seemed like hours as Dawn and Darryl became like Siamese twins locked together by the hips and lips. Darryl helped Dawn with her studies as she helped him work on his thesis for his major, which was Dawns favorite subject, History. Darryl had concentrated on the early 1800's as he had always been fascinated by the Cowboys and Indians era. Once Dawn had told him of the real history of her people, Darryl became even more enthralled with the many different tribes and mainly of the Plains Indians. He was so deep into his research that he would miss practice occasionally as his coach wouldn't mind snatching his butt up out of the library to remind him of such. Dawn would only giggle and continue the research for him, as she knew he was torn between the two. He had even expressed to her his desire to learn her native language of Algonquian. The Spirits surely had her confused as to what road to travel. Her heart knew of only one road at the moment and that was a road to true romance and happiness. She would pay the price some other day, but not today. She would live for the moment and a truly wonderful moment it was with her Darryl.

Occasionally Dawn would call home to give her inquisitive and worried mother the *Low Down*, as KD phrased it, on the school and her studies. She knew she had to pay special attention to her words to her mother. Her mother's insight was only second to her father's. She could always read Dawns mind even through the phone by listening closely to her voice and words. Dawn thought her parents to be truly psychic at times. It pained her to be so deceptive towards people she loved and respected with all her heart. She thought it best for them to meet Darryl first so they could see his eyes and know his spirit before they would judge his...heritage?

While Darryl was at practice Dawn found herself alone in her room as her mind cascaded with disturbing thoughts on her present situation?

Surely my parents wouldn't be so...ancient? No, of course not or I wouldn't be here. Would I have to be with a man I care nothing for in my heart with the notion that I would come to love him with time. How terrible it must have been for the women of ancient ways. Yet, how could they have known another way if that were the ways of all people? They would no doubtlessly consider that they were lucky to be wanted by such strong young handsome Warriors. The settlers brought many new ways and thoughts to this land. My parents showed much wisdom in allowing me a future among them and a future of helping all our people. Yet my heart is heavy as I deceive them willingly. They deserve better from the one they raised and nourished so honestly and passionately. I must let them meet my lover, my life, my Darryl by winter's end for it will be soon when our greatest Warrior will ask for my father's blessings to join with his only daughter. I will speak to Darryl of this soon.

CHAPTER 5

The big Game

"WelcoMe, college FooTball fans, to the Rose Bowl. I'm your play by play anchor Jim Wheeler and with me calling the first college championship game of the new millennium is my co-anchor Bob Dickinson. Bob, the USC Trojans haven't seen a championship game of this magnitude in some years. We hope to see a challenging game from them with the likes of their star quarterback Trevor Tregoning," said the announcer to his co-anchor.

"Yeah, I know what you mean Jim, I'm going to have my eye on their quarterback The Ju, as well. They don't call him that because he's Jewish," replied Bob.

"That's right Bob. He earned that nickname by immolating the famous Johnny Unitas. They just used Johnny's initials for short. We expect to see him put it on the line this game."

"Hey Jim, what about that wide receiver that just made his mark with the play of the day last week?"

"Oh yeah, let's not forget about The Mongol, Bob. He help to put them here in the Bowl."

"Well I think that's The Mongoose Jim and he definitely deserves an honorable mention from that upsetting game against the UCLA

Bruins. They weren't expected to pull that one off against an undefeated team."

"But they were on their home front and sometimes that makes the difference Bob."

"Your absolutely right Jim and that is definitely not an advantage they have here in sunny Pasadena."

"Well, it's kick off time and The Wisconsin Badgers has lost the toss. USC will receive the first championship kickoff of the new millennium. We will be back with live play by play coverage from the Rose Bowl in Sunny Pasadena, California here on ABC."

"And…cut to commercial. Hey Jim, you're not going to ruin this broadcast with all that new millennium crap are you?" asked the director of productions.

"Yeah Jim, give it a break man," said Bob laughingly.

"Bite me, the both of you!" exclaimed Jim as the whole set burst into laughter. Embarrassed, he ducked his head down to pretend to go over a few of his notes on the players.

Darryl and dawn stood just outside of the Trojans designated locker room embraced in each other's arms.

"Shouldn't you be outside for the kick off, Love?" Dawn asked concerned for the game but at the same time not wanting to let Darryl go off to get possibly injured.

"I guess so but I'm on the Special Teams. They won't need me until The Drive. I have time for one more kiss for luck," replied Darryl with his usual debonair smile.

"Look at you Mr. Greedy. You already have enough luck from me to last you a whole NFL career."

"But they are a really good team and you know what this win will do for my career."

"Okay you, you're lucky I like it so much too," said Dawn as she gave in to a tender heartfelt kiss from the love of her life.

Darryl donned his helmet and ran back on the field as Dawn couldn't help but notice how well his buttocks looked in his uniform which was much tighter fitting than the baggy jeans he wore all the time. She followed behind to find her seat with her best friend KD.

Suddenly, the closing of a locker room door startled Dawn. As she turned around she could recognize the quarterback Trevor and started toward him to wish him Luck and to throw in a good word for Darryl. She hoped that if she told him that Darryl was in great spirits and in the best shape of his life then The JU would throw him the ball more. It would probably be a naive gesture but she couldn't help herself, as she just had to be there for her man. Dawn suddenly gave pause as she noticed that Trevor wasn't alone.

Trevor stood in the dark tunnel like hallway, which led to the opposing team's locker room. Dawn didn't recognize the black suited man as anyone connected to USC. She found it strange that the man wore dark shades in such a dimly lit area. She had no idea what they were talking about but she could sense that Trevor was upset about something. She found herself uncontrollably moving toward them. The mysterious looking man had an Italian Mafia look to him as she remembered the many gangster movies she used to watch with her mom. Luckily, Dawn's eyes were directly on him as she instinctively darted behind a stanchion when she spied his head turning in her direction. Fortunately, she was not noticed and now she was even close enough to hear their conversation.

"Look, you tell them this was not the deal!" said Trevor forcefully but as quiet as he could possibly be and still get his point across.

"These are not people you bargain with, especially when they already own your sorry ass. You gave away your bargaining options when you sold your soul to them your junior year. They look at it now like they are doing **you** a favor. You can either accept their offer and get rich or decline and lose everything. Your life; your choice," said the mysterious man in an eerily calm voice.

"Motherfuckers!" exclaimed Trevor not caring to hold his tone as he sped off to join his teammates. He felt he had no choice as his mother was in a cancer ward fighting everyday for her very life. His father had divorced her and had left them years ago. Her mediocre job barely covered the medical bills. Time was running out and he knew there were never any guarantees to land an NFL contract.

Dawn pressed her back firmly against the stanchion she was hiding behind in fear of being found as the two men departed the hallway. When the way was clear she quickly went to find KD to tell her of her suspicions.

Dawn immerged from the locker room entrance squinting her eyes to adjust to the bright sunlight but too nervous and anxious to stop. Suddenly she was snatched back by a strong hand around her wrist. Her heart jumped into her throat, as she knew it must be the *mystery man* and he **did** see her. To her delight it was only KD.

"Girl, don't do that!" snapped Dawn as she gave KD a small punch to her shoulder.

"Ouch! What was that for?" asked KD, in more shock than pain that Dawn hit her.

"Ah, quit being such a baby. That was only a love tap," said Dawn with a smile of relief and then a hearty laugh, when she had looked into KD's eyes.

"I know those aren't blue contacts you have on. Girl, you're much too pretty to do that. I love your brown eyes," said Dawn so lovingly, KD gracefully removed them.

"Girlfriend we have big trouble and I'm going to need your help," said Dawn with a serious tone.

After a quick explanation Dawn and KD sprinted down to the field to talk to the coach.

"What if the coach is in on it too, Dawn?" asked KD.

"I didn't think of that. What do you suggest?" "What do you think of your man? You think . . ."

"Don't you even go there!" Dawn abruptly interrupted.

"Okay then so we let Darryl know and just leave it up to him. Deal?"

"Deal," said Dawn in agreement.

Dawn and KD could hear the crowd roar as they headed toward the sidelines. The game was well under way with the Trojans already ahead by 6 points from a kickoff return of 92 yards. Darryl was on the sideline hoping for a turnover when he could hear his name being called. He turned around to see Dawn and KD gesturing for him to come over to where they were standing. As soon as he was in earshot, Dawn told him what she had secretly witnessed. Darryl wasn't sure what to make of what Dawn may have thought she saw, but he knew of the big money that was at stake with college and pro football games. Even the alumni had betting pools. Unfortunately there is always someone not willing to rely on luck to win. Especially when there were millions at stake.

"Thanks baby, I felt that Trevor was a little on edge. I just thought he had a few jitters from the pressure of being the team captain. But when he didn't seem excited about that great TD right off the bat . . ." Darryl paused as the crowd went into a roar.

"Alright! Good job Omar baby! We got the extra point. Hey, peep out The Ju," demanded Darryl of Dawn and KD as they watched Trevor act as if the kick was missed instead of good.

"You see, that's what was tripping me out. If you didn't tell me about him, I would have dismissed it," said Darryl.

"You think we should talk to the coach?" asked Dawn as KD nudged her for asking something they had already agreed was not a good idea.

"No, we can only trust the other players with this because it's our careers that's on the line. Everybody who's anybody is out there watching and making their draft pick list as we speak. Taiwan just secured himself a place in the NFL with that 92-yard kickoff return. Man, he must have broken three tackles on that play. That cat is illusive as hell. That's why we call him 9 Lives and he just used up 3. KD, didn't you used to date him last month?" Darryl inquired jokingly.

"Yeah, he was tattoo number five," replied KD.

"Honey, you better figure out another way to cheer yourself up when you are depressed or you're going to run out of places to put those tattoos," said Dawn to make light of the situation.

"Well there's always body piercing," said KD as they all laughed. "Don't worry I got this Boo," said Darryl as he kissed Dawn and went back to the sideline to talk to each teammate one on one.

The game went on as expected with a pretty even defensive match up. The Trojans normally would have had a more talented offensive line up but with Trevor in the pocket calling the shots they could only catch what was correctly thrown at them. Darryl knew he was playing a great game and was even able to catch some throws that he knew he wasn't meant to catch. He was convinced of that when he checked out The Ju's reaction after each surprising catch. By the 4th quarter it was obvious to the whole team what Trevor was doing. They had to take him out the game to secure their 3-point lead over the Badgers.

In the huddle Darryl winked at the center Jimmy (Wimpy) Wendall. Wimpy whom got his nickname from the cartoon Popeye because of his love for cheese burgers in turn winked at the left guard Todd (Big Will) Williams. Big Will, always on one knee because his back would hurt to bend over, turned to his right and gave the right guard Eddy (The Ghost) Murray a slow nod.

With the play called and just after the break, Darryl gave his fullback Shane (The Dane) Mosley a tap on the butt to signal him to pay close attention to the ball. Darryl didn't want to inadvertently because what Trevor was trying so desperately to accomplish by causing a turnover from a fumble when they let The JU take a couple of bad sacks. The Dane was always there to protect the quarterback like a Great Dane or Pit Bull in the event of a Blitz. He would normally run the ball for a few added yards for first downs, but for the first time in his college career he will let happen the unspeakable. Today he will let the opposing team into his leader's office and ransack it to the max and that they did after the snap. The Dane saw it coming in slow motion as he leapt for the ball, as The Ju was the unfortunate recipient of a brutal simultaneous tackle from the Badgers defensive ends. The Dane recovered the fumble without missing a stride and started down the sideline towards the goal line. Darryl was right on his heels and when The Dane took a clip to the shin from cornerbacks' feeble attempt to stop him it was just enough to trip him up. As The Dane was about to eat turf he spotted Darryl just in front of him and decided to fake a fumble which he hope would put the skin square in his chest which it did and Darryl found himself surprisingly in the in zone. He was so excited he forgot to do his victory dance as his teammates rushed him and tackled him to the ground in excitement. The Game was over and as Darryl was raised into the air by his teammates he could see Dawn, but she was looking downfield. When he looked in that direction he could see Trevor The Ju still sitting on the turf with his head between his legs. He would have some soul-searching to do over the next few months, but only if he survived The Mafia Family's wrath.

CHAPTER 6

Spring Break

Darryl anD Dawn was in deep conversation about their plans for Spring Break.

They had Dawn's dorm room for themselves as usual this Friday as KD had already started her break and was most likely with some guy on his motorcycle riding the Boulevard in a lime green Bikini.

"You know my father wants me to bring that Heisman Trophy home during our break," said Darryl playfully as he pulled her close to him.

"Uh … ah, don't you even try it mister. That Trophy is staying with me. You know what it means to me. You gave it to **me** and besides it looks too good on my dresser," said Dawn as she pushed herself away from Darryl and stood guard in front of the statue.

"Well that's fine Dawn, I don't mean for you not to be by my side when I go home for Spring Break."

"But I thought we talked about you meeting my parents at the reservation?"

"Yes we did but we didn't say when, baby."

"Well my parents already sent two tickets that was supposed to be for me and KD, because if I told them about you then ... well, you know," said Dawn with disappointment.

"You see that's exactly what I'm talking about!" said Darryl with anger as he took a moment to calm himself and continued, "Your parents are going to blow a gasket when they get a load of me in all my glorious Blackness. That will not be a fun, stress-relieving break for me at all, Dawn. I don't know, maybe if they had a heads-up at least. Do they even know that KD is ... well, you know ... KD?"

"Of course they don't and I didn't expect it to be an issue. But I knew from the moment that I accepted this ball, that **you** would definitely be an issue," said dawn as she scooped up the ball from her bed and lightly tossed it to Darryl to bring home her point.

"Well I don't think I'm ready to be looked at like I stole something of great value from your people for days on end. Now if you come to my home it won't be like that at all. Well, my ex may give us a little drama but I can handle her crap. Anyway, I already have bus tickets for the noon coach to South Central, LA. Here's your ticket. I hope you will meet me there, Dawn," said Darryl as he put one of the tickets on the dresser and used the trophy as a paperweight for it.

As Darryl turned around to face Dawn she had already went into her book bag and pulled out an airline ticket.

"Here," she said as she handed him a ticket and continued, "My flight is at 12:30 PM and I too hope **you** will be there. I will have the trophy and you can tell my tribe of your victory as a warrior on a Field of Battle called Football," said Dawn hoping to bring a smile to Darryl's grim face.

"Well I guess this is our first official fight," said Darryl. "No, it's more like our first disagreement," replied Dawn.

With that, Darryl departed after a somewhat cold kiss between the two. Both with the hopes that the other would give in and surprise them at their departure point.

With her bags packed and ticket accounted for, Dawn was ready to catch a cab to the airport. She was waiting till the last minute to pick up the phone to call for a cab in hopes of receiving a call from the Darryl.

Dawn was startled for a moment when the phone rang just as she went to pick it up to call for a Cab. She quickly became excited as she picked up the phone.

"Hello, Darryl?" Dawn inquired.

"No, It's me silly. Just wanted to wish you a safe trip home. I know you can't wait to get there," said KD.

"Oh, well thank you. I will call you when I get there."

"You be Careful in that airport. There are a lot of bad elements hanging out in there waiting to pray on an innocent little thing like you. I take it you are alone?"

"I hoped not, but I guess so," said Dawn with sadness.

"I knew he would chicken out; the big wuss. How can men be so brave in the sports arena and be afraid as mice when it comes to matters of the heart is beyond my comprehension. Tell you what girlfriend, you and I have a date with the tattoo parlor when you get back," said KD knowing how to cheer Dawn up.

"Okay, you've got a date!" said dawn with conviction.

"Oh my goodness, you serious Dawn?" asked KD reverting back to Ebonics.

"You damn Skippy!" said Dawn with a serious attitude.

"Girlfriend, I'm scared of you. But let's do this! See you when you get back. Love you."

"Love you too and thanks," said Dawn as she pressed down the receiver button without a pause to call for a cab.

Dawn couldn't help, as much as she tried, to keep from looking back at the phone in hopes that it may just ring out of sheer mental persuasion because she willed it to do so and have her man on the other end. But the ring never gave birth and she departed with a sigh of sadness.

"Darryl! Yo man, Darryl!" yelled Darryl's roommate Big Will, trying to get his attention as Darryl seemed to be off in a daydream.

"Oh, I'm sorry Will. What were you saying?" asked Darryl awakening from his intense thoughts.

"Man, didn't you say your Bus was at noon?"

"Yeah, so what time is it anyway?" inquired Darryl still somewhat out of it.

"Man, you are the only one I know that will have a watch on his arm and still ask for the time. You kill me with that shit dog. Man, you got about a half hour before your sorry ass will be walking back to Compton or East LA wherever the hell you're from," said Big Will with a smile. He was only giving Darryl a hard time to keep him real after such a tremendous season that he knew would surely put Darryl in the league of NFL first round draft picks.

"Yeah right man, I got to get it together. It's just that I couldn't sleep last night after I got back from Dawn's," explained Darryl.

"Don't tell me. Woman troubles right?"

"Is there any other kind?" asked Darryl sarcastically as they both laughed.

"Yeah, we spend half our life trying to avoid them and the other half trying to pursue them. Then somewhere in the middle we catch one or one catches you depending on your point of view. Anyway, you better hope that she's The One or you're in for one hell of a ride," said Big Will.

"You got that right my man. I got a call from Moniqya last night when I got back from Dawns'. Man, she's been on my Tip big time ever since the game against UCLA. I was hoping she would get the point when I didn't return her calls. But I slipped last night and didn't check the caller ID first thinking it was Dawn. When picked up the phone and heard her voice, I went blank," said Darryl angry with himself for losing control.

"Bad move my man. But I hope you straightened her out because quite frankly I'm tired of making excuses for you. Hell, she's been calling here damn near every day since the Bowl."

"Nah, she caught me at a bad time, Bro. All I could think of was to agree with everything that she said just to get her off the phone in case Dawn called about coming to **South Central** with me," said Darryl with emphasis on his hometown to answer Big Will's ploy earlier.

"Man, I know where you're from. I was just busting your balls. Keeping you real, dog. Anyway, it sounds as if you have some serious soul searching to do," said Big Will showing concern for Darryl's situation.

"Your right and I'm going to do now what I should have done last night." Said Darryl as he picked up the telephone receiver. After several rings and no answer Darryl slammed down the phone in anger.

"Shit! I waited too late. God, I don't believe this."

"Man you got it bad, Dog. You better jump in one of those cabs that are usually at the gate and get your sorry ass to that airport before she gets away.

You let her go home like this and she may return married to that Indian guy you were telling me about."

"I was thinking the same thing. I'm out. Hold down the Fort, Dog," said Darryl as wave of anxiousness overwhelmed him. He gave Big Will a quick hug.

"Good looking out, Todd."

Big Will stood frozen, silent and quite shocked at Darryl's behavior as he never seen him like this in the four years he knew him. But he knew what love could do to a man or woman for that fact and he just dismissed it and thought to himself, *"man does he have it bad!"*

CHAPTER 7

The Passing

Darryl counted his lucky stars as he opened the back seat door to a cab just outside the campus gate entrance. He threw his backpack and duffel bag in the seat and hurriedly closed the door behind himself.

"My man, take me to the airport and step on it!" demanded Darryl of the cab driver.

"Yeah, Yeah that's what they all say but no one wants to tip worth a Goddamn. So we get there, when we get there, okay Buddy," snapped back the elderly looking cabby.

"You don't understand man, I can't miss this flight. My girl is counting on me to be there," said Darryl pleadingly.

"Look pal, I don't know what your problem is but your life won't be over just because you missed a flight with your girl. I don't know what it is with you kids these days. Everything is hurry, hurry. Now where I'm from . . ." the cab driver paused to check both ways as he came to a stop sign.

"Look man, would you just go for God's sake!" snapped Darryl as the cab driver took too long to continue through the stop sign.

"Let's here wait a Goddamn Minute College boy!" snapped back the cab driver as he turned around to look Darryl square in the eye. But then he gave pause and inquired, "Don't I know you son?"

"I don't think so, sir," said Darryl now giving the cab driver a little more respect now that he was looking him in the eye.

"I never forget a face and I sure as hell seen you somewhere before. I just can't put my finger on it right at the moment. What you say your name was?"

"I didn't sir but it's Darryl, Darryl Jackson."

"You shittin me! The Darryl Jackson that won the Heisman?"

"Yes sir," said Darryl proudly but without conceit.

"I can't believe it, Darryl the Mongoose Jackson in **my** cab. I told my boys at the Mason lodge you would be MVP and get that Heisman. Everyone thought it would be the Ju who would get it, but man he played like shit the last few games and you stepped up like a pro. Man, if I didn't know any better I would have thought he was trying to throw those games or something. Anyway, what the hell is a superstar like you doing in a cab? I bet there are a thousand ladies on campus ready to ride you to the ends of the earth if you wanted them too."

"That's just it, I only want one woman and she's about to get on a plane alone and I can't let her down like that. It would mean the world to her if I were there by her side. I was being selfish and I screwed up. I just need to make it right. You know what I mean. She may be The One."

"Well that must be some special lady you got there. By the way, my name is Allen Creed and I have a need for speed. So let's put the pedal to the metal, my man," said the cab driver. Their heads angled back from the abrupt acceleration of the Ford LTD. Darryl smiled as for the first time he felt the dividends of being a celebrity and the hope of being with his girl in her time of need.

As Dawns' cab was stopped at a stoplight she could see a greyhound bus pass through the intersection. She couldn't help but wonder if that was the very bus that Darryl was traveling on. She looked at her watch and saw that it was only a quarter to twelve. She smiled and thought of how he must be sitting on the bus now bobbing his head to some fresh beats, as he would put it.

When the cab stopped again she noticed a tour bus pulling up beside them and thought again of her man and what he must be doing. Then she thought what if he called while she was on the phone with KD. While she was pondering this thought she turned to look out the window and right before her eyes was the Bus terminal.

"Stop, Stop!" yelled Dawn at the cab driver as she began to frantically point in the direction of the terminal. The cabdriver, use to this kind of gesturing, calmly slowed down his vehicle and turned into the Greyhound terminal. Dawn quickly paid the driver and ran inside. She looked in her pocketbook and fished out the ticket Darryl gave her and found the bus to South Central. Before she went through the gate to the bus, she gave the terminal one last look just in case Darryl wasn't on the bus yet. To her satisfaction she turned toward the bus in search of her man.

"Hurry up lady, you just made it. We are under new management now and they are hot on us getting out of here on time so let's get you onboard," said the bus driver. He checked Dawns ticket and placed her luggage in the baggage compartment. Dawn could only giggle to herself as she boarded thinking of how surprised and happy Darryl will be to see her on the bus. As she started towards the back of the bus she could hear the driver close the doors and announce the next stop. Dawns heart started to pound heavy in her chest as she neared the very back of the bus still not spotting Darryl. She felt her internal body temperature rise to a fever pitch as she found herself in the back of the bus now and Darryl was nowhere to be found.

"Lady, can you please find a seat. I can't take off unless everyone is seated," said the driver over the mike. Dawn was now in a panicked state as she turned around to find every soul on the bus staring at her with malicious contempt. All she thought to do was to sit down and pray for a miracle. Dawn sat there alone hoping Darryl was just running late. Her fears overwhelmed her as she felt the bus move in reverse out of the terminal. She began praying that Darryl would come banging on the door and fall into her loving arms exhausted. She thought of how tight she would hold to him and never let him go the whole trip. But she found herself pulling her feet up with her knees to her chin in a fetal position with tears rolling down her cheeks as she was on a bus all alone at full speed with a one-way ticket to South Central, LA.

Darryl thanked Mr. Creed for risking a speeding ticket to get him to the Delta terminal with a couple of minutes to spare. He found it amusing that the driver, Big Al as he asked him to call him, wouldn't accept payment from him. He couldn't help but wonder what would have happened if they were stopped by a traffic cop. He probably would have been able to get Big Al off with just a warning had the cop recognized him. But he quickly dismissed that thought as to not allow himself to get caught up in that superstar mentality. He had seen too many good players lose sight of reality and think because they are extremely highly paid professional athletes, they were above the law. He had just read how an elite Football pro had been sentenced to two consecutive life terms with no possibility of parole for a double homicide. No other name was mentioned in the stabbing of the two victims but the Linebacker from a prominent NFL Team. Now instead of him trying for a Super Bowl ring, he will be trying for his Freedom the rest of his Life in prison.

Darryl reached the departure gate after a quick jog through the airport with a minute to spare. He couldn't help but think about the O. J. Simpson commercials he used to watch growing up as a child. But he quickly dismissed that thought as he remembered the Trial of the Century and how some days he would think O.J. innocent and others he would think of him guilty as hell. He felt a sense of anxiety to realize that very soon he would be just as famous or as infamous. A smile came to his face as he walked down the gate tunnel to the plane as he thought of Dawn.

"*If I just stay focus and true to Dawn everything will be just fine,*" he thought to himself as he entered the plane.

"You sure like cutting it close don't you. Welcome aboard sir, you are the second to last passenger unaccounted for," said the Airline pilot as he motioned to the stewardess to close the plane's door.

"Thanks, it was a last minute decision. But I'm glad I made it," said Darryl as he walked pass the First Class section. He immediately spied the coach section as soon as he opened the dividing curtains in search of Dawn. He felt a sense of panic come over him as he reached his assigned seat to find the adjoining seat empty as well. He took a quick scan of the cabin making sure to make eye contact with each person as not to miss Dawns beautiful face. Deep down inside he knew that she was not in the cabin because she would have been all over him by now. But his mind couldn't accept the fact that she just wasn't on the plane. "Miss, excuse me Miss!" exclaimed Darryl at the Stewardess oblivious at the fact that she was right in the middle of her Safety instructions to the passengers.

"One minute Sir, this is very important to know for your and the other passengers safety," replied the stewardess politely but firmly to maintain control of her cabin.

Darryl sat down and was made to buckle his seat belt as another Stewardess motioned him to do so. She then placed his carry-on bags in the overhead. The plane was now cleared to taxi to the runway and was in the process of doing so. Darryl then remembered that there was one other person unaccounted for and now to his dismay he realized that it was Dawn. His feelings turned from anger to fear as he began to wonder what had happen to the love of his life and was she safe. At the moment all he could do was to stare out the window with his mind riddled in turmoil as the Jet engines revved it's 5,000 pounds of horsepower to thrust the Boeing towards the heavens. A tear rolled down Darryl's left cheek as he somewhat heard the Captain talking about the plane's cruising altitude. But all he could do was close his eyes and pray for Dawns safety as the plane was now leveling off on a one-way glide path to Dawns Home Town, of Pierre, South Dakota.

CHAPTER 8

The Jacksons

Dawn was In no hurry to depart the bus once it had pulled up to the terminal. The sights around the city, as the bus made it's way to the South Central Station, were disturbing to Dawn. All the other passengers were off the bus now. Dawn slowly removed her bags from under her seat and the overhead bin. She thought it wise to bring her bags on the bus after another lady had complained of someone trying to take her luggage instead of their own, during one of the rest stops. She felt a tremendous weight as she walked down the aisle towards the exit. It took a moment for her to realize that it wasn't the weight of the bags she felt. But it was the heaviness of the weight she felt on her shoulders, as Americans like to say. Today that metaphor was correct because her heart was heavy, as it has never been before. All she could do was put one foot in front of the other and pray that the Spirits haven't yet abandoned her.

Dawn managed to crack a smile, as the Driver thanked her for using their Business, just as she exited the bus. She didn't know what would await her at the end of the terminal lane just beyond the gate. She hoped it would be a familiar face and welcomed arms. Hopefully Darryl's, but at this point, she would take what she could get.

"Here, I will get that for you miss," said the bus driver as he opened the door to the lobby for Dawn.

"Thank you sir," replied Dawn as she walked through the entrance stopping at the door to let the driver ahead of her. She thought if she stayed close enough to him that she would be safer. Dawn gave pause as she spotted what seemed to be a family still waiting impatiently for someone whom obviously didn't get off the last set of buses. Before she realized it, the driver was out of sight and she found herself without a potential escort. She decided to approach the family as she recognized Darryl's mother from the picture he kept of her on his dorm room desk.

"Hello Mr. Jackson, Mrs. Jackson," greeted Dawn making sure to speak to the Father first, as was her tribe's custom.

Dawn looked them all in the eye with every bit of courage her heart could muster. She didn't even look down when Darryl's mom postured on her much as KD did when they first met. That seemed a long time ago to Dawn now as she continued, "I'm a close friend of Darryl and I was hoping he took an earlier bus home. I guess you are looking for him too," said dawn worriedly.

Darryl's mother was a tall dark skinned woman that looked quite young for her obvious age to have an oldest son a senior in college. She didn't wear what Dawn now realized were extensions from living with KD. She wore her hair natural. But there was something familiar about her features that Dawn couldn't quite put a finger on. She quickly dismissed the thought when she realized that there was an extra person among them that had to be Moniqya by the way she was staring her down like a Vulture ready to pounce upon its prey.

Darryl's mom noticed the beautiful smile on Dawn's face dissipate as Dawn had turned her eyes towards Moniqya. She was rather an expert at preventing attitude before it reared its ugly head. She was a high school teacher and she could spot a potential ugly scene a mile away. Her expertise was math but she definitely spent more time dabbling in the fine art of Public Relations. She quickly stepped in, "It's nice to meet you, ah . . ."

"Oh, I'm sorry. I'm Dawn Whi . . ." Dawn paused as to not want to give away the fact that she's a Native American. *What would my ancestors think of me now? My Father. Am I ashamed of my heritage? Have I stooped so low as to deny who I am for the acceptance of a family I don't even know? Spirits forgive me.* Dawn decided the price too high to pay.

"White Cloud, Dawn White Cloud," said Dawn as she raised her head with pride.

"It's a pleasure to meet you too. Darryl talks well of his family. He was very eager to be home this week. I don't know what happened," said Dawn as she began to worry about him.

Darryl's Father, a handsome man with some premature Grey peppered throughout his hair and beard, put his hand on Dawn's lean shoulder to comfort her. He could feel the concern in her voice for his oldest son and he could also see the fear in her eyes to be away from him in such circumstances.

"It will be alright, Dawn. My son is a survivor like his father. He will be just fine and I'm sure, as soon as he can, he will give us a call."

Darryl's mother saw innocence about Dawn that made her feel a truth in Dawns words as she's never experienced in a person before. She was so use to people saying one thing and meaning another; she unconsciously became pessimistic about everything she would hear. But now for the first time since her husband asked her to marry him, she believed Dawn's words to be true.

Mary turned to her husband Charles and motioned to him to go, in a sign language only couples married for many years could do. She couldn't help but notice that Moniqya was not showing the concern for Darryl that Dawn so convincingly portrayed. It seems all she could feel was contempt for dawn as it flustered all over her face with her eyes red now from holding back the rage she obviously felt inside. Mary walked between Dawn and Moniqya as her husband, the gentleman he was, carried Dawn's luggage to their car.

Moniqya felt a warm liquid running down her fingers. She was shocked to realize that she was so angry she had dug her freshly manicured fingernails into the palms of her hands drawing blood as she clinched her fist. *This Bitch must have lost her mind to think she can just waltz her narrow ass in here a steal my man! She needs to take her Red ass back where she came from. God's my witness, next time I see blood it will be hers.*

CHAPTER 9

The Cheyenne's

As The plane made its decent over the South Dakota landscape, Darryl suddenly realized that this was actually his first flight. He gripped the armrest in a sudden panic as he felt the plane banking right. His fear subsided as he looked out the window to the most beautiful and tranquil sight he had ever witnessed. It was spring time at home but here he could see glorious snow-capped mountains with lakes abound which glistened like diamonds from the reflections of the sun. He imagined what it would have been like to grow up in a place like this. Would he too have known the innocence and peace that Dawn wears so well? This he could only ponder as the plane touched down and taxied to the terminal.

Darryl had his seat belt unfastened and was ready to depart the plane long before the door was opened. He barely heard the Captain and stewardess thank him for flying their Airlines as he darted past them and into the gate lobby. He eyed a set of phones already in use and as he turned to look for another set, he spotted Dawn's Family. Standing there, he could see that Dawn's Father was much larger than his photos showed him to be. He had a worried look on his strong bronze face, which conveyed to Darryl that he hadn't heard from

Dawn as well. Dawn's mother, keeping her head high still, portrayed a smile of desperate hope.

She and Dawn could have been twins, with the same striking features, average in height but slender with strong broad shoulders. Long thick straight Raven black hair adorned her as it did Dawn. She wore the same moccasins too. Her dress was very traditional, as were the Beads around her slim neck. They all wore beads. A hell of allots of beads for that matter, Darryl thought. Even the earrings they wore were made of feathers and beads. Dawn's Father, Chief Red Moon, looked exceptionally sharp as the bright red, white and purple beads accented off the Black Satin like shirt he was wearing. He had on tall white boots with tassels of white and red feathers streaming from the top as his jeans were pushed inside of them. But what was truly impressive was the thick white belt and gold buckle Chief Red Moon wore with obvious pride. It was something Darryl remembered seeing the Champion Rodeo riders wearing when Dawn drugged him out to see a bunch of cowboys on horses a month ago. He thought of them as being a bunch of Red Necks at first, but then as the show went on, he realized that they were the bravest bunch of men and women that he had ever witnessed. The Football field couldn't even come close to what even a Rodeo Clown would have to brave. Darryl thought that he would take a charging Running back over a Raging Bull any day.

Darryl wanted so desperately to call back at the dorm and find out what had happened before he approached Dawn's family. He knew her Father would want answers. He felt a shiver going down his spine as he remembered a story Dawn told him of her father.

It was twelve new moons ago when my Father and I were fishing on the Reserve Lake Sesquite at Sioux Falls. A young Indian by the name of Little Tongue galloped up to Father and told him that his horse was stolen by another Indian called Many Feet. Father went in search of Many Feet on his most trusted and cherished steed. Everyone thought that when chief Red Moon had caught up too Many Feet it wouldn't be a pretty sight. Indians still believe in the fact that there's honor in death. Some still try to live as the ancients had but most have conformed to the Western ways. Had it been the old days he would have brought Little

Tongue not only his horse but the horse of Many Feet as well. Darryl grimaced as he remembered what Dawn had said to him next… *He would have also scalped Many Feet just to make a statement to the rest of the Tribe. Fortunately for Many Feet My Father has adopted some of the Western Worlds democratic philosophy. He took time to question him about the horse of Little Tongue. It didn't take long for Red Moon to find out that Little Tongue had lost his horse to a game of 3 Card Molly. When my father learned of this he felt betrayed. Chief Red Moon caught back up too Little Tongue and well, now they call him Crooked Tongue.*

Darryl shook his head vigorously hoping to flush out the feeling of anxiety he was feeling towards approaching Dawn's family. Remembering that story only worried him more of Red Moon's reaction to know for sure, that his daughter was definitely not on that plane.

"Chief Red Moon!" yelled Darryl from across the Lobby.

Red Moon looked at his wife Fawn Running Deer and then at his son Black Wolf. They didn't acknowledge his look of puzzlement, so he knew they did not know of the stranger that seemed to know him. This gave Red Moon an odd feeling he knew he didn't like. His expressions always showed his true inner feelings and right now it was very evident to Darryl that he better do some fast explaining.

Darryl put out his hand as he reached Red Moon. Red Moon stood in silence with his arms crossed staring deep into Darryl's eyes. Darryl in return kept his eyes in direct contact with Red Moon's as Dawn's mother reached out to shake his hand. This was a gesture that would have been unheard of back in the 1800's. But Red Moon showed no dismay at his wife's actions.

"How do you know us, Sir?" asked Fawn with a worried look.

"I attend USC with your lovely daughter, Dawn," said Darryl as he took his eyes off Red Moon to great Dawn's mother. Darryl could see Fawn's eyes light up just to hear her precious Dawn's name rolling off his tongue. Darryl immediately returned his vision in the direction of Red Moon whom didn't express the same emotion. He seemed to show more concern for Darryl and the role he played in his daughter's new life among the Americans.

"You know of my daughter, young man?" asked Red Moon of Darryl.

"Yes Sir, ah...Chief," replied Darryl as he noticed Black Wolf moving on his right flank to come behind him. He stood his ground.

"Dawn was supposed to be on this flight. I got on at the last minute. Man, it blew my mind that she wasn't on the plane! I was just about to call back to the dorm to see if anyone had seen her." Darryl looked straight into Red Moon's eyes and continued, "I'm worried about her too."

Red Moon gestured to his son to back off his ambush on Darryl. He will practice again the art of diplomacy and give this African American that has just come into his lifeline a chance to prove his honor.

"Then let us not hesitate to make that call," said Red Moon. "Well it looks like the phones are all used up," stated Darryl as he did a visual search of the lobby.

"This will not be a problem." Red Moon nodded his head at Black Wolf. Black Wolf walked over to the concession stand where a middle aged Indian worked. He pointed at Red Moon and without hesitation they motioned over Darryl. Darryl realized the clout Chief Red Moon must have possessed, as Red Moon never as much turned around to look at the vendor.

Darryl had no luck when he called the dorm so he decided to take the opportunity to call home to let them know of his changed plans.

CHAPTER 10

The Understanding

Dawn coulD sMell the distinct aroma of Soul Food slithering from the kitchen like a Cobra on the attack of some unsuspecting prey. Mary was hard at work, *if you could call it that for it was her greatest joy*, at putting the finishing touches on dinner.

Charles watched in amusement at the funny look on Dawn's pretty face as she caught a whisper of an unusual aroma.

"We call it Chitlins darling," contributed Charles with a smile. "Chitterlings, Dad. Mother always cooks it for Darryl when he's been away from home awhile," said Melinda with her nose turned up so far Dawn could see the clip on the bottom of the diamond nose ring she was wearing.

Dawn could see the close resemblance of Darryl and his sister. His younger brother Earl was about the same height and build as Darryl, but he was not as dark in complexion and had features closer to that of his mother. She thought that Darryl definitely had more of his father in him than anything. Now the unusual smell became more predominant to Dawn.

"Chit-ter-lings?" inquired Dawn anxious to know why the smell was so poignant.

"Yeah Child, Chitlins," said Charles as he threw a frown in Melinda's way as if to say *"Don't you dare correct me child with your wanna be proper ass."* Melinda took the hint but threw back a frown of her own. "It's the intestine of pig, you know, Hog. Mother also likes to throw in a little maw as well. Now that's the stomach of hog. You see Dawn; African Americans became experts at preparing delicacies such as this many decades ago. They pretty much had no choice because they were making due with what they were savagely given. It's amazing what they managed to gracefully prepare with pig parts like ears, feet, snout and Lord have mercy the damn head. Well we call it Soul Food and believe it or not we eat it now because we actually want too," explained Charles to a fascinated Dawn.

"Well some of us don't want to eat that crap. Don't ask me to waste my time by your bedside when you all have heart attacks either," said Melinda as she started to set the dinner table.

"Ah shut your hole, oh crazy girl with that vegetarian nonsense. Your grandmother live to be 92 eating this way all her life," snapped Charles.

"Yeah, and she died of a bad heart too now didn't she?" snapped back Melinda.

"Alright now, don't sass me girl. I'll go old school on ya and whoop that 19-year-old butt of yours. I brought you in this world and I'll take ya right out."

Dawn was amazed at how Melinda was able to converse with her father in such a manner. Neither showed respect for the other but there was a strong aura of love and unity in the air. They seemed to be at play with one another. Meaning what they say but at the same time not meaning what they were saying. All she knew is that she understood.

"Yes, I understand. We too have dish similar, but we use fish and deer intestine in a sun ripened tomato stew. We call it Bopese. It's my Father's favorite," said Dawn with a smile suddenly feeling homesick and anxious to call them, but too shame to ask.

"Well I bet that can stink up a house quick too," said Charles with a hearty laugh.

"Actually, mother always cooks it over an open pit along the riverbed. The huts we use are more for just sleeping only."

"You all got a problem with my cooking?" asked Mary as she placed the crock-pot of chitterlings on the dinner table.

"No Mam! I was just . . ." Dawn paused as she looked back to see Mary waving her off with a smile. Mary's eyes were lit up like beacons of light, as she gave witness to a young adult showing total respect for the elders. Dawn immediately understood that she was just playing with her and this gave her a warm feeling to know. She felt part of Darryl's family at that moment.

Dawn exhaled a sigh of relief and for the first time today she actually felt comfortable and most of all, safe. With that came a terrible price; Hunger. Dawn realized that she hadn't eaten all day and the aroma pouring out the kitchen amplified that bottomless feeling in the pit of her center.

Fried chicken, smoked ham-hock collard greens, sweet water cornbread, Chitterlings and sweet potato pie battled to take over Dawn's third sense. The Chitterlings won by a landslide. The Collards came in second and the Cornbread fell in last. They would soon battle again for the control of Dawn's first sense as soon as the food was blessed and Jesus was thanked.

Dawn sat at the dinner table with Darryl's family and thanked the spirits that Moniqya wasn't invited. She thought Mary must have had enough insight to know such a situation should be avoided at all cost. Dawn was amazed at the wonderful gold-rimmed China and silverware that adorned the mahogany table. She had noticed that the China cabinet was also made of the same rich dark hardwood. Quite frankly, she was astounded at how beautifully the house was decorated and well-kept compared to the seemingly run-down exterior. Dawn thought it a shame that people wouldn't know, of the great house Darryl's parents had, from the looks of it outside. But then again, maybe that was the point.

Just as Charles was in the middle of saying grace, the phone rang abruptly, startling everyone.

"I'll get it, just go ahead and dig in," said Mary as she graciously stood up to answer the phone. She paused just a second to overlook her table like a Drill Sargent inspecting her well trained, polished protégés. The table was fit for a king and all was looking sharp, even the sweet potato pie with its crown of roasted walnuts and lightly browned mini-marshmallows was standing proud. Mary gave her dishes a nod and a stern smile of pride as she pivoted right to answer the phone.

"…And God Bless this food we are about to receive, Amen," finished Charles as he slapped Earl's hand back from grabbing the bowl of cornbread.

"Ladies first, oh knuckle head boy," said Charles in disappointment of his son for he had thought he taught him better manners.

"Hello, Jackson residence," answer Mary as she looked back at the dinner table to make sure everyone was indulging themselves in her soulful cuisine.

"Hey mom, it's me, Darryl. How you doing?" asked Darryl excited to hear his mother's loving voice.

"Hey baby. I'm doing fine. Hey yall it's Darryl! Baby what happened to you? Where are you? You know how worried you had us? Boy, if you ever scare me like that again . . ."

"Okay, okay mom, sorry. It couldn't be helped this time. It's a long story and I don't have time to get into it. I just wanted to let you know that I was all right and that my plans had changed. That's all I can tell you right now, Okay."

"Yeah right, well I got your changed plans right here."

Darryl's mouth dropped open in shock to hear his mother speaking such language.

"Mother, what would reverend Bridger say?" snapped Darryl as he pictured his mother holding her crouch as the boys in the hood did when they used that phrase.

"Quit tripping, oh crazy boy. I'm not talking about that. Here Pooky, let me put someone on for you," corrected Mary as she slapped back Charles hand from trying to grab the receiver.

"Damn, woman, he's my son too!" exclaimed Charles as he abided by his wife's wishes as if he had a choice.

Dawn giggled at Darryl's pet name as she excitedly placed the receiver to her ear.

"Hello, Pooky," whispered Dawn laughingly as she couldn't believe it was the love of her life on the other end.

"My God, Dawn? Hey you guys, it's Dawn!" yelled Darryl as even Red Moon raced to the phone.

"What are you doing **there**, baby?" asked Darryl as his heart raced with anticipation.

"I wanted to be with you so badly and the Spirits guided me to the Bus station, but you were not on the bus. I was so afraid Darryl, but now I'm with your great family and my spirit is at ease. I love you so much. Where are you?" asked Dawn as tears flowed uncontrollably down her full boned cheeks.

Mary felt a swell in her throat to hear the sincerity of Dawns words to her oldest son. She was as happy as any mother would be to know her son had found such romance and true love.

"I love you too, Boo," replied Darryl reluctantly and somewhat under his breath as to not allow Red Moon to get wind of his heartfelt words.

"You are not going to believe this Dawn, but I'm in South Dakota at the Pierre airport with **your** family. Here, I will let you talk to your Father. You can imagine the expression on his face right now."

"Yes I can, so you better put him on quick," agreed Dawn as she braced herself as to compose her emotions.

Chief Red Moon's eyes lit up for the first time that day as Darryl cautiously handed over the receiver to Red Moon. He could hear Red Moon greeting Dawn first in their native tongue and then Fawn had been handed the phone to do the same.

"Well, that's quite a story Dawn. Why didn't you call to tell us of your Darryl?" asked Fawn lovingly.

"I knew it would have disappointed you and Father. I was hoping to let you see his eyes, witness his smile and come to know his spirit as I have," explained Dawn.

"We understand and you would have done well to do so. We have much to discuss. For now, you rest your weary soul and come to know your adopted family. They will be a significant part of your lifeline now. We will take care of your Darryl. I can tell that your father feels a strong aura about him as if he has a place among us.

He will no doubtlessly come to prove his worthiness in the coming days. The Spirits willed this to happen so I will pray to them for you to overcome your tribulations as well," said Fawn showing wisdom beyond her 35 years for she had had Dawn when she was a mare sweet 16.

"What do you mean Mother? Am I to stay here?"

"Yes dear, it is the will of the Spirits or you would have been here embracing us at this very moment. You have an inevitable bonding among the African American community now that must be acquired and maintained. It will be a difficult road but it is a road our ancestors have chosen for you to walk. I know you will not fail. Remember your up-bringing, be always true to your heritage and all will be well."

"Okay mother, I will. Give Father and Black Wolf my love," said Dawn as she felt a prideful tear drop from the tip of her chiseled nose. "Be safe on your journey little one and don't worry, we will help to guide your Darryl on his journey as well," said Fawn as she slowly placed the receiver on its cradle.

CHAPTER 11

Dawn's Trial

"LooK are you guys going to help me out or not? I've been waiting on that son of a bitch for 4 damn years and I'm not about to roll over for that Pocahontas bitch," said Moniqya to her old crew.

Cassandra (Killa) Patterson was the new leader of the Disciples. She was in deep thought as to what she could get out of Moniqya's plans for Dawn that would benefit her and her crew.

"Look Bitch, don't bring your ass in here trying to regulate. You had your reign and you gave it up for that same motherfucker that's dissin your sorry ass. Now you bring your tired ass in here talking your shit. Bitch you must be out your damn mind. If you had tried that quitting shit with the Crypts, you'd be one dead ass bitch right now. So why the hell should we help you? What's in it for us?" asked Killa as she pulled her braided hair up into a ball atop her head which signaled to her pose' that it was about to be on up in here.

Moniqya knew she had to talk fast and well to get help from the Disciples. Killa's posture was heightening, as she was becoming very agitated. Moniqya quit as the gang's leader 2 years back to prove her loyalty to Darryl, hoping he would think that she changed her ways. She knew the relationship was over even then, but the prestige of being married to an NFL player was too great for her to voluntarily let go.

"Look Killa, I get rid of her and I'm back with Darryl. He's into the Family thing, so all I have to do is get pregnant and I'm in the house. After he signs a contract I'm sure I will find a way to break you off something. You have my word on this as a Disciple."

"Bitch, you ain't no damn Disciple!" exclaimed Dianne, another member of the crew, to whom went by the name "Weps" as she was an expert in weapons due to her short hitch in the Army.

"No Weps, once a Disciple always a Disciple," corrected Killa as she nodded to the rest of her crew and then to Moniqya to signify an agreement.

Moniqya sighed with relief as they sat around a table to make plans to get rid of the significant threat keeping her from landing a good man with boundless potential.

"I don't want her dead. I just want her to look like a chump. You know, scare the hell out of her and send her crying back to wherever the hell she came from. Darryl swears by his family, so I stayed close to them. That bitch is over there right now and I can't allow her to fuck up my flow," said Moniqya.

"Okay, I feel you Moni," said Killa reverting back to Moniqya's old call sign as she was called due to her uncanny ability to squeeze big money out of any situation. "Let's work out the details over dinner, ladies. Moni's treat."

Moniqya and The Disciples cased Darryl's parent's house over the next few days for an opportunity to catch Dawn alone. No such opportunity came and Moniqya found herself too impatient to wait any longer. She thought every moment she waited would undoubtedly place Dawn closer to Darryl's family.

"Fuck this shit! Let's do this," said Moni as she jumped out of Killa's Low Rider. Perturbed at Moniqya's impatience of deviating from their agreed plan, but remaining somewhat loyal, Killa and the others followed her lead. Moniqya walked up behind Dawn as she and Melinda were walking to the corner store.

"Bitch, you got some nerve!" snapped Moniqya as she grabbed Dawn's arm and swung her around.

Killa and her crew stepped in between Dawn and Melinda to keep her from helping Dawn. Melinda had to be held back as she tried to intervene once the initial shock of the moment had subsided.

"I always knew your black ass was no good!" yelled Melinda at Moniqya.

Dawn stood her ground as she had suddenly realized that her journey has just come to a terrible storm and if she was to weather it out, she must confront it head on or be washed away and consumed by it.

"You have no honor. Your spirit is weak and you will never know inner peace as long as you greed for material comfort," said Dawn in such a calm tone her words rang with wisdom to those around her.

"Fuck you and all that red ass Confucius bullshit!" screamed Moniqya as she lunged at Dawn grabbing her throat with one hand while trying to pull her to the ground by the hair with the other.

Dawn flashed back at her childhood when she used to wrestle with her brother and his friends. She remembered how her brother taught her to not fight the motion of falling. By allowing yourself to fall, you could control the way you land and use that same flowing motion to bring down your opponent. This Dawn did and the results were more than she had hoped. As she tucked her head under, she hit a rolled on her shoulders, using her legs to help bring Moniqya plummeting down behind her. Moniqya was so surprised and startled that she didn't have time to react as she literally ate the pavement with a hard bone-chilling Thud.

"Oh snap!" exclaimed Killa as she and her crew bent over Moniqya in awe of the blood oozing from her mouth as she lay there oblivious of consciousness.

"Damn Pocahontas, Oh girl is knocked the fuck out! I never like her sorry ass anyway. Let's go ladies. Our business is done here. Nice move Pocahontas," said Killa as she and her crew departed leaving Moniqya sprawled out on the ground.

Melinda helped Dawn to her feet and said, "Dang girl, you're stronger than you look."

Dawn thanked her ancestors for the craft they handed down generation after generation. For it was the art of making moccasins that gave Dawn such strength in her upper body as she would help her mother to soften deer hide by rubbing it for countless hours on a granite stoned pole.

"We must help her," said Dawn still showing compassion much to Melinda's surprise.

Mary and Charles drove an embarrassed and shamed Moniqya to the county clinic. All Moniqya could do was stare in the window at her toothless reflection. She knows she has lost the respect and trust of Darryl's family. Which in turn means she had lost the respect, trust and love of Darryl, if she ever truly had it in the first place.

CHAPTER 12

The Tribe

Darryl ThoughT To himself that the scenery before him had to be the most beautiful and tranquil he had ever seen in person. He took in every awe-inspiring sight with a youthful smile. His head resembled that of a little puppy dog sticking out the back seat window. If he had a tail it would be wagging furiously with wild abandon. He could see the sign ahead announcing the crossing of the reservation. It reminded him of something he would see at the crossing of a state line boarder.

"So how big is this reservation?" asked Darryl of Black Wolf whom was also sitting in the back seat of the Red Moon's jeep.

"When I was but a pup we had over 5,000 acres stretching North to the Badlands, West to the Rocky Mountains and South as far as the Black Hills, but now we barely have 1,000. Most of this land was turned into National Forest of one kind or another. They let us hunt on them but we can no longer build upon it," said Black Wolf solemnly.

Darryl was lost of words as he realized that he had hit on a delicate subject among Dawn's people. The closer Red Moon drove to the inner town the more run-down the area had become. He was expecting a resort like haven, but he quickly came to realize that Dawn's people were barely surviving from the looks of the dwellings.

The sun was starting to set as it had taken a couple of hours to reach Dawn's home from the Pierre International airport. The setting sun spell bounded Darryl, as he couldn't take his eyes off of it. He was so lost in his thoughts he was oblivious to Fawn addressing him.

"I said it's beautiful, isn't it?" yell Fawn trying again to get Darryl's attention.

"Oh, I'm sorry Mrs. Running Dear," replied Darryl as he embarrassingly turned to face her.

"Please dear, call me Fawn. We don't use the mister and miss's titles among our people. Actually it wouldn't work given the nature of our names. It's a story I shall tell you some day, but for now please come in and have dinner with us."

Darryl entered the modest dwellings of Dawn's family. He immediately inhaled a familiar aroma. A smile came over his face as he remembered his mom's cooking and how he wish he were home right now with them and especially Dawn. That would have been wonderful he thought.

"What are you smiling so for?" asked Fawn of Darryl.

"Oh nothing. It's just that I thought for a moment that I smelled Chittlins. It's my favorite. Mom is probably putting some in the freezer for me right now."

"I'm not sure what that is, but I think you would like it if it **smells** like anything you may have eaten before," said Fawn curious of the similarities between Native American and African American recipes.

Darryl sat down to a feast of Bopese, sweet yellow corn, fried fish, yellow rice, corn bread, roasted sweet potatoes and sugar fried bananas. He thought to himself that the only thing missing was the collard greens but there was a kale dish that proved to be a decent substitute.

Darryl thanked Fawn for the wonderful dinner and followed Red Moon to a trail that led to the riverbed where there was a roaring campfire surrounded by elderly Native Americans.

"Elders, I would like to bring a young man into your Life-Circle. He is of My Dawn's Lifeline and the Spirits has placed him among us. I would challenge anyone to deny him the rights of passage!" bellowed Red Moon as his words pierced the hearts of everyone within earshot. Suddenly a horse galloped up with a haunting figure straddling it.

"I deny this man any such passage! He has not proven he deserves a place among us. He is an outsider that knows nothing of our people. Chief Red Moon how could you even entertain such an outlandish idea?" exclaimed Brave Heart, son of Chief Running Bear of the Sioux tribe.

"Do not question Chief Red Moon my son. He has an insight that even I have failed to fully obtain. We must give this young man a chance to prove himself as we did those that had come before him. It's not up to us to decide his fate. It is only for the spirits to decide," interjected Running Bear.

"All right then, have it your way. I hereby challenge this right to passage with a duel!" snapped Brave Heart.

"Woe, Hold on a minute here Chief! What the hell is going on? Who is this...this man and what does he have to do with me?" inquired Darryl confused to all that was happening before him.

"News around here travels fast, especially when there's a stranger within our midst. No doubt the Sioux vendor at the airport heard our conversation and called ahead to Chief Running Bear after we left. The warrior abound that great steed is Running Bear's oldest son Brave Heart. He is to receive Dawn as his wife this summer. He had proved himself worthy last winter and had no one to challenge him for my consent. He no doubtlessly would have no remorse if you were dead," explained Red Moon as he placed his hand on Darryl's shoulder to show support.

"That was a challenge of many black suns ago, Brave Heart. We are not here to entertain such a challenge. We are here to decide his worthiness to walk among us," said Red Moon.

"What's with this **challenge** thing, anyway?" asked Darryl of Red Moon.

"You would have had to do battle with Brave Heart of his own choosing. We had many ways to settle this, long ago, some more deadly than others. If you had proved victorious, you would have become part of our Warrior Cast and be highly honored among our people, as Brave Heart is our strongest Warrior. You would have had no resistance in wedding my lovely daughter Dawn."

"And if I did not defeat Brave Heart?" asked Darryl solemnly? "Then you would still be honored through your bravery for trying, if you had survived the ordeal."

"All right! So be it. Then I challenge his rights to passage. Look at him. He can no more ride a horse than I can fly a plane!" Bellowed Brave Heart from atop his mighty steed, as the Sioux Elders laughed.

Darryl stared at the mighty girth of Brave Heart, mounted proudly on his salt and pepper stallion. He looked like a true Indian, straight out of a Western movie. But this was no movie and the characters were real, much too real.

Brave Heart dismounted and sat at his father's side waiting for Darryl's response to his challenge. Chief Red Moon, remembering his promise to Dawn, Motioned for Darryl to sit down beside him. They were all around the fire as it crackled and snapped loudly as air escaped the cherry wood that was ablaze.

Red Moon yanked off the pouch that hung around his neck. The elders all gasped at first like they had never seen him do such before and then started talking among them. Darryl strained to hear, but all he heard were mumbles as he watched Red Moon pack his pipe tightly. Whatever he was packing in it, had to be very important because he seemed like he wanted not to waste a drop. He handed, the now tightly packed pipe, to Darryl, much to his dismay. Darryl looked deep into Red Moon eyes, that were now glistening red from the glow of the raging fire or maybe not. He felt the sense of fear subsiding as a replacement of anxiousness overwhelmed him. He fearlessly took hold of Red Moon's precious pipe and placed its chiseled end to his lips.

"You would know your answer after you have finished the contents of this pipe, Dawn's Darryl," said Chief Red Moon as he pulled a stick out of the fire. Its end still red hot, he lit the pipe as

Darryl inhaled deeply with reckless abandon. He watched Darryl's eyes closely as the Elders and Brave Heart looked on in awe at the mysterious effects of Red Moon's secret herbs.

Darryl's eyes were wide with anticipation of the smoke now enveloping his lungs to come bursting forth with a horrendous vengeance. He swallowed and much to his delight, it was as if he had just swallowed clean air. He couldn't believe that he even attempted such a thing but it was something reassuring in Red Moon's voice that made him trust him whole heartily.

Suddenly, Darryl found himself floating as his legs stretched back out from the Indian position he was sitting in. He was standing in front of the fire now alone. Night had turned to morning and all was quite accepting for the blissful song like tones coming from the edge of the river.

CHAPTER 13

Darryl's Ancestors

Darryl walKeD To the edge of the river where he saw a young Indian woman washing clothing with river water. She turned around and smiled at Darryl as if she knew him. Darryl couldn't help but feel that he knew her too. As he got a little closer he could see that she resembled an old photo his father once showed him of his great grandmother, but this woman was much too young. "Great grand?" asked Darryl.

"Great grand! Charles, what have you been drinking? Son come here and help your mother pull out these clothes," demanded June.

June was light brown in complexion as she was a descendent of full-blooded Cherokee Native Americans. Her hair was a long and wavy dark brown with streaks of silver. Her features were strong as her cheeks rose high and full and her nose long and narrow with a slight bend at the tip. Her eyes were so light that some days they seemed hazel and others a light brown.

Darryl, still confused, but compelled to help, walked over to the very edge of the bank. As he bent over to pull the clothing from the river he was startled by his own reflection. His face was that of his grandfather's or at least a much younger version of Charles senior.

He was so mesmerized by his own reflection that he bent down closer and then even closer until he slipped and fell into the river. The flow of the river washed him downstream until he was hit over the head with a rope.

"Grab on son!" yelled Narosi as he started tugging at the rope as Darryl held on for dear life. Narosi's arms was like steel as he had been a slave most his life. He had the curse of a Mandingo build, which branded him a life of fighting other slaves as White men bet on the outcome. He was also used for mating to produce more of the same. He never minded the mating but what he did mind was the loss of his offspring as they were sold to other slave owners. He swore he would never lose another of his children long as he lived.

Darryl reached the bank and crawled completely out of the water as Narosi helped him to his feet.

"Thanks, ah…Father." Darryl looked up in awe at the tallness and powerful build of Narosi.

"I thought I taught you to swim better than that, my son? We have more work to do, I see. Put on some dry clothes and meet me at the stables," said Narosi as he wound the rope up in loops, trying not to show the disappointment he obviously felt.

"Yes father," said Darryl as he headed toward the house to change. He had felt he could swim, but he had panicked and did not know how to tap into that ability. He felt that he didn't belong here. He paused, confused. Suddenly he felt his lungs fill with a substance he couldn't recognize. Memories came flushing in and he started to feel as if he belonged once again. He dismissed the substance as water he must have inhaled during his momentary lapse of knowledge. Yet he still wondered why for a moment he thought he was someone else.

In the coming hours that turned to days and days that turned to months, Charles learned of horseback riding from his mother and hand to hand combats from his father. He was told of his Cherokee heritage by June and of the Ethiopian legacy his royal ancestors left behind before being destroyed and enslaved.

Charles and Narosi sat at a campfire and conversed about Narosi's past. He had told Charles how he had been left for dead after a fierce battle between himself and another Mandingo called

Assuzi from the Tribe of the Nairobi. June's father found him, while he was out hunting for food. Narosi had been badly beaten and was left to die. Running with Elk had taken him in and painstakingly nurtured him back to health. He had fallen in love with Running with Elk's Daughter June and was allowed to unite with her after he proved himself worthy.

Charles couldn't believe his ears at what his father had endured for the rights of passage. He had grimaced at the sight of his father's chest as he could see where they had hung him by his chest with hemp rope tied to Eagle claws till he broke free. He was reassured that it was well worth it, which he could see, as his parents were literally inseparable.

"Father, I must confess. I haven't been myself of late. I've been having this strange feeling of belonging somewhere else, ever since that day I fell in the river and forgot how to swim. I thought I just hit my head on a stone but I've been having these weird dreams too," confided Charles to Narosi.

"I've come to believe in the Spirits, as your mother believes and I feel that you will know all when the Spirits allow you to know all. Till then, have patience and just enjoy life as it is given to you, my son," said Narosi as he threw another piece of wood on the blazing fire. As the wood hit the flames it seemed to burst into a ferocious ball of fire. Charles covered his eyes with his right forearm as the flames seemed to blind him. When he uncovered his eyes he found himself in the midst of several elderly Indians.

"Welcome back, Dawn's Darryl," said Red Moon standing and bending over to help Darryl to his feet.

"What the hell!" exclaimed Darryl as disorienting memories came rushing back into his mind like the waters of Niagara Falls.

"Enough of this nonsense! What is your answer?" revered Brave Heart of Darryl.

Darryl leapt over the roaring fire with the ease of an Elk as he mounted Brave Heart's mighty steed with a single bound. The horse raised up in protest but Darryl took hold of its flowing mane and instantly the horse knew who was in charge. He turned the horse towards Brave Heart and rode full gallop at him. Brave Heart, true to his namesake, attempted to stand his ground, but ducked at the last minute as Darryl jumped the powerful horse over Brave Heart and the Raging fire.

Darryl side straddled the horse and began to do acrobatic moves as the elders looked on with amazement. Brave Heart looked on with severe contempt. As Darryl swung the steed back around he picked up a spear that stood in the ground and lunged it at Brave Heart while still in full stride. Brave Heart stood his ground, as he was embarrassed at his last attempt of bravery. He counted his lucky stars as the spear landed at his feet.

"There is your answer!" snapped Darryl as he dismounted and handed Brave Heart his steed.

"You will regret this Day," said Brave Heart as he and his Father mounted his horse and sped away.

Darryl turned to red Moon with a puzzled frown. Red Moon only put his hand on Darryl's shoulder and said, "One Day you will understand how our ancestors leave within us all they know, all they are. We have but to tap into our inner minds to summon that which is they and join it with that which are we. Come, you still have much to learn before your Rights to Passage begins at dawn."

Darryl followed Red Moon back to the cabin. He would sleep well tonight after his training and he will dream of his Dawn.

CHAPTER 14

The Chosen One

The aroMa oF eggs, bacon, pancakes and what he would come to know as partridge, awoken Darryl. He gave pause at the moment to remind himself that he was not at home.

"The sunrise is more beautiful than the sunset. I still can't get over how fresh the air is here," said Darryl as he sat down among Dawn's family for breakfast.

"Yes dear, things must seem very different here than where you are from," answered Fawn as she began fixing Darryl's plate.

"If you plan on seeing many more sun rises and sunsets, you must pay close attentions to my words Dawn's Darryl," demanded Red Moon.

"Woe there! Hold on Chief. I don't mean any disrespect, but this Dawn's Darryl thing is getting out of hand. It's just Darryl or hell, you can even call me Mon-G."

"What is a Mon-G?" asked Red Moon with a puzzled frown.

"It's just a nickname the fellows call me back at the U. Have you ever heard of a Mongoose? Well, I'm as fast as one," said Darryl showing a little conceit. Red Moon seemed not to take it too well as he had stood up and walked away from the table. Darryl became perplexed and had spied Fawn and Black Wolf as to detect a clue from their expressions.

No such luck, as Fawn and Black wolf continued eating as if nothing had happened. Darryl thought maybe he was just over reacting and had convinced himself to continue eating as well. He began to reach for his fork when . . .

"Oh Shit!" Whelped Darryl as Red Moon walked up to him and threw a Rattlesnake at his feet. Darryl raised up abruptly and stumbled backwards over his chair. He hit the ground with a thud and began scrambling backward away from the snake, its tail rattling with fierce anger. Darryl watched in awe of Red Moon as he bent down close to the rattler, waving his left hand in a figure eight motion. Suddenly, he snatched the rattler with his right hand just below its head.

"This fast?" asked Red Moon of Darryl.

Darryl got to his feet, now realizing the seriousness of his situation grabbed the snake out of Red Moon's hands. Darryl swung the snake to the ground in such a manner it spun around like a whip. The rattler soon composed itself and started toward Fawn. Darryl sped toward the snake and before it could draw Fawn's blood in a deadly strike, Darryl had snatch it up by the tail as if catching a fumbled football and had the snake in a whirlwind spin over his head.

Darryl looked Red Moon squared in his eyes and spiked the ferocious reptile to ground with a deadly thud.

"That fast!" exclaimed Darryl.

"Good. You may be The One. Only the Spirits can tell for sure, but you have a special ability like I've seen in no other man, that was not one of us," said Red Moon looking deeply into Darryl's eyes.

"What do you mean by The One?" asked Darryl of Red Moon. "Our people believe that there will be a deliverer much like your Jesus that will help to guide our people back to their past glories. We are a proud people, but most have given up and succumbed to gambling and alcoholism. We were promised so much in the past and now we are paying a higher price than we ever imagined possible. You posses a deadly combination of ancestral power within you, **Mongoose**," explained Red Moon as Darryl proudly listened on.

"With the proper guidance, you can be our savior, the greatest Warrior ever blessed by the Spirits. Do you believe Mongoose? Do you accept Mongoose Walking Proud?" asked Red Moon of Darryl.

Darryl looked at Red Moon, then at Fawn and lastly at Black Wolf. He thought of no place and no one he would rather help. He thought of the sacrifices that he would have to make. He thought of this new race of beings that he had come to know. He thought of his ancestral heritage that was almost lost and how finding it again was so important to him. He thought of the humanities so many of us had lost for the sake of progress. He thought of the extraordinary price that we have all paid for that so called progress. Most of all he thought of his Dawn and how even as screwed up as the world may seem at times, there still seems like a little innocence can find its way through it all.

"I would be honored to be considered a Great Warrior among you, Chief Red Moon," said Darryl as Fawn Hugged him tightly, tears of joy streaming down her lovely face.

Chief Red Moon picked up a war spear and raised it to the Spirits and bellowed at the top of his voice in his native tongue, "Spirits hear me, Chief Red Moon, I send forth Mongoose Walking Proud this day as our salvation! Guide him well, this day of his trial, if he is to be **The Chosen One!**"

Darryl had felt pride when he accepted his Heisman trophy, but it didn't hold a candle to what he was feeling right now. There was no scale yet invented that could measure neither the immense magnitude of pride nor the weight of burden he felt this day. He would be known among the Native Americans now as Mongoose. A creature fast and agile enough to catch snakes, scorpions and lizards. Mongoose Walking Proud of two worlds that seem as far apart as the Grand Canyon, yet as close as Siamese twins when all the "Bull" was washed away.

"Come Mon-G, we must meet with Chief Running Bear and his son Brave Heart to discuss The Trial," demanded Red Moon as he kissed and hugged Fawn. Black Wolf followed Red Moon and Mon-G to the camp of the Sioux tribe.

CHAPTER 15

The Trial

Mon-g was aMazeD once again at the great amount of respect Red Moon possessed on the reservation as he witnessed the Elders standing when he entered the large tipi. They had sat in unison, around the small fire inside, as Red Moon sat to show respect for him as their Chief. Darryl took a squat next to Chief Red Moon.

"Have you decided, among you, a fitting Trial?" asked Red Moon of the Elders.

"We have decided on the Peak Trial," answered Chief Running Bear as Brave Heart stood in agreement. Darryl attempted to respond in kind as Red Moon placed his hands on his shoulders to keep him from fully rising. Darryl sat back down in an Indian position as Red Moon stood himself.

"This is a dangerous time of year for such a Trial. The spring winds are softening the snow on the sacred mountains. Black Hills is in an unstable state. It would be suicidal to venture it these new suns," pleaded Red Moon.

"It sounds to me as if you are willing to give honor away for free. Many have died to prove them worthy to be called Warriors among us. Are we to soften our ways of honor for an outsider?" Snapped

Brave Heart at the Elders but mainly directing his anger towards Red Moon.

"I, Mongoose Walking Proud of Cherokee descent and now of the Cheyenne, accept the Peak Trial this day!" snapped back Mon-G as he stood to square off on Brave Heart.

"Chief, what the hell is a Peak Trial?" asked Mon-G of Red Moon under his breath as to not allow the Elders to hear.

"I will explain later," replied Red Moon with teeth clinched as to not allow his lips to move.

"Then it is done. Let the preparation begin," said Running Bear as all the Elders stood and walked out the tent.

"The terrain to the top of the Black Hills is treacherous with the snow melting as it is. An Avalanche has the force to uproot even the deepest earthen tree. You must trek to the top, where you will place my War Spear among the others you will find there. You will travel there and back with a young Warrior guide of your choosing. You must return to this camp with one of the other spears you will find on the sacred ground."

"Okay easy enough, but something tells me there's more to it than that. Are there any rules? You know, can I hire a helicopter and just fly there and back?" asked Mon-G making light of the situation.

"The Warrior guide is there only to show you the way. He would not be in a position to help you find the sacred grounds. You must find it of your own cunning and tracking abilities. If you are to survive this Trial Mon-G, you will have to tap into your ancestral powers," said Red Moon as he placed his right finger to Mon-G's heart and then to the center of his forehead.

"Thanks for the vote of confidence Chief, but I've learned a thing or two in that dream-state you put me into. You know Red Moon; you should really bottle that stuff. You'd make enough loot to clean up every reservation in America," said Mon-G clownly as he and Red Moon departed the tent.

The young Native Americans standing before Mon-G looked to be of 25 through 30 years of age, but he knew them to be a mere 16 through 18 years old. He thought how rough a life they must have endured with the burdens of becoming Warriors. They had persevered and were truly considered worthy of such in the eyes of their fathers. Black wolf was among them. Brave Heart was not as he was by his father's side kneeling down with his eyes on Mon-G.

"Choose your guide well Mongoose Walking Proud," said Chief Running Bear.

Black Wolf eyes were aglow with pride, as he knew Mon-G would surely choose him on such an important adventure. He nodded in agreement as he spied Mon-G looking directly at him.

"I have made my decision," said Mon-G as Black Wolf stepped forward with confident anticipation.

"I choose Brave Heart!"

The Elders gasped and started to talk hurriedly among themselves. Mon-G peeped out Brave Heart, as his eyes were twice their normal size. He was looking at the mountains now with a new perspective. Brave Heart was slow to rise, like his legs were all of the sudden made of straw. He locked his knees and had composed himself as he raised his strong chiseled chin proudly. Brave heart walked to Mon-G and looked him square in his stern eyes. Mon-G stood his ground as he had dug his feet firmly into the dirt as to brace himself for a not so unexpected blow.

"I am the last warrior you should want as a guide, unless you wish to be guided to the Spirits," said Brave Heart as he pointed towards the heavens.

"That's exactly why I choose **you**. It would make my victory all the sweeter," said Mon-G with his usual debonair flair.

"I accept as guide to Mongoose Walking Proud. May the Spirits guide us well," said Brave Heart as to not show any animosity towards Mon-G.

Mon-G went to a sulking Black Wolf and placed his hand on his shoulder. Black Wolf looked up at Mon-G confused and embarrassed. "You have nothing to be disappointed about young Warrior. You have already proved your worthiness and shall not die with me this day.

My Spirit would never rest if I come to take you from your parents and beloved sister Dawn."

"I understand Mon-G. Here, you will need these," said Black Wolf as he handed him his gear.

"Be weary of the one they call Brave Heart, Mon-G," said Black Wolf worriedly.

"Don't worry, my father once told me to keep my friends close, but always keep my enemies even closer. Something tells me Brave Hearts bark is much worse than his bite," said Mon-G reassuringly.

CHAPTER 16

The Trek

Mon-g ManageD To crack a smile as Chief Red Moon handed him his most cherished War Spear. Mon-G had noticed that it was the same type of spear he used to hunt with, during his dream-state.

"This Spear is familiar to me Chief," said Mon-G.

"Yes, there are many similarities among our people that I'm just coming to realize as well. One must wonder if that is by design or by nature."

"Maybe it's by nature and the design is for our people to never realize it," replied Mon-G gazing over the wonderful workmanship of the Spear.

"How true. Hmmm...You have true insight my young Mongoose. Use it well and be wary of the one called Brave Heart. He has honor so he will guide you well, but he knows he will lose Dawn in the process."

"I know and that is why I will keep him close to me. Thank you for your teachings. I will do you and the Cheyenne proud or die trying. Let Dawn know of this day and what Mongoose Walking Proud has sacrificed for her love and for her people!" bellowed

Mon-G as he mounted Red Moons mighty steed and road off with Brave Heart.

Brave Heart led Mon-G to the edge of The Black Hills and dismounted. Mon-G followed suit as he felt a rush of anxiety overcoming him.

"Man, it sure didn't look this high from the reservation. So what now?" asked Mon-G of Brave Heart.

"I will take you to the midpoint Ranger Station where I will wait for your return. You must bring down a different Spear so I will know that you indeed made it to the sacred ground."

"How will I know my way from there?"

"There's no trail at that point. You most make your own trek using the gear you have there and the prowess of your tracking and hunting abilities," said Brave Heart as he pointed to the bag Black Wolf had given him.

"Hunting abilities?"

"Yes, you will most likely come upon a wolf or bear or two."
"You've got to be kidding me. How far up are the other Spears?
How can I track my way to them?"

"The signs of others traveling the same path has been covered by snow. The Spirits dwelling the sacred grounds will summon you. If you are the one, you will be given signs. You can turn back now if you wish. Believe it or not, it's a far cry better than the Sun Dance ritual for the rights of passage for becoming a Warrior."

"Okay let's do this," said Mon-G with confidence as not to let Brave Heart see him sweating his challenge.

The trek to the Ranger Station was treacherous at best. Mon-G and Brave Heart had stopped numerous times to catch their breath and rest. Mon-G had thanked the Spirits that he had an athletic background. He needed every bit of every conditioned muscle in his body to continue. He gave a sigh of relief as Brave Heart motioned to stop just once more before reaching the Ranger Station.

"Let us rest before we trek the last leg of my part of this journey. I must admit, I do not envy you this day, Mon-G," said Brave Heart.

"Yeah man, you should have saw your face when I picked you. I was a little worried about you, but you seem to be an honorable man, Brave Heart."

"I too was worried about you destroying everything I hold dear, everything I've worked so hard to achieve, Everything I am."

"I can get behind that Brave, but I'm not here to destroy you or your way of life. I just fell in love with the most perfect woman any man could imagine. I think she loves me as well. If she decides to be with you, then so be it. But I will do everything within my power to show her that I am true to her devoted love. Even if that means I have to give my life over to the Spirits in the process."

"Then let us go forth Mongoose Walking Proud and claim your glory for your people and mine," said Brave Heart as he started climbing over a fallen tree that lay across the trail. Suddenly a branch broke under Brave Heart's foot. He reached out to grab one of the other branches and fell back as it snapped. The tree started to slide down on Brave Heart as the snow under it gave way. The mighty oak followed brave Heart as he slid back down the steep slope. Mon-G had side stepped as the tree had passed him with the quickness of his namesake and had started running behind the tree which pickup up several smaller trees as it avalanched upon Brave Heart.

"Spirits give me strength! Make my footing sure!" cried out Mon-G as he pounced upon the mighty oak and grabbed its branches as reigns. He tapped into his power of sight and spotted a large boulder a few yards off the trail. The tree gave a sudden pause as it collided with a deeply rooted pine. The abrupt stop sent Mon-G in an Eagle dive and his prey was one Brave Heart, as he managed to grab his arm and pull him behind the boulder.

"I got you buddy. Stay down, that tree is on the move again," demanded Mon-G as he watched the tree hit the boulder with a deafening thud and fly over their heads.

"You alright? Anything broken?" asked Mon-G.

"I guess I'm more embarrassed than hurt. It seems I'm bruised but it could have been worst. Thanks."

Mon-G helped Brave Heart to his feet. They walked toward were the tree had disappeared and were surprised at why.

"What the...!" yelled Mon-G as his mind tried desperately to catch up to what his eyes were witnessing. The view was magnificent yet terrible as he and Brave Heart realized that they had slid off the trail and was within yards of the edge of a cliff.

"I guess you saved my life," said Brave Heart solemnly. "It was nothing you wouldn't have done for me."

"What is more important is the fact you were able to achieve such a feat. Even I would have been at a lost for such a rescue as that. You have opened my eyes to a great possibility."

"And what is that Brave Heart?" asked Mon-G curiously. "That you are The One."

Brave heart shook Mon-G's hand with a grip that told Mon-G of his convictions. They continued up the mountain not taking for granted the tormenting terrain.

"Hey Darryl, there is the ranger station up ahead my man. I'm going to chill there while you go on up ahead," said Brave heart to a wide eye Darryl.

"You son of a bitch. What the hell happened to your Native accent?" asked Darryl in amazement.

"Man, you just don't know what it's like to be a Native American these days. You couldn't even imagine what I go through on the reservation on a daily basis.

I never had anything against you nor do I care to marry Dawn if she's not in love with me, But they expect this from me and it's just easier to play along than fight their customs and beliefs."

"Well you sure fooled the hell out of me. But you seem pretty intelligent, Brave. Why don't you attend college like Dawn?"

"Just as you are doing this rites of passage to belong, I too feel obligated to do as the Elders wish of me."

"That's a shame because I see so much potential in you, Brave." "Then you are the first American to do so. You See Mon-G, it is easier for me to change my views of you and your people than it is for you to change your views of me and my people."

"I don't think that is a true statement of most African Americans, Brave," corrected Mon-G as he sat down on the log Brave Heart had sat. "That's exactly what I am talking about. You have a separation among the Americans. Each culture and religion can say they are different for one reason or another. But the Native American culture is lumped into one equal sum. The equation is that we are all alike no matter what the tribe. Yet we are as diverse as any other people, sometimes even more so."

"I never realized that. I wonder why that is so," said Mon-G feeling guilty of his ignorance.

"It is because we have not a soul these days to represent us. The proud Americans of African and European decent have always had many men and women to recognize their efforts in developing this country to become the most powerful free States in the world. The Malcolm X and Martin Luther King era was a classic example of your diversities as a people. They showed that your people could be as ruthless or as peaceful as you wished to be. Native Americans, Indians, have always been branded as ruthless."

"I never quite looked at it like that before, Brave, but your right. We do need to take a step back and reevaluated your people's present situation. I promise to do all I can to make a difference," said Mon-G as he placed his left hand on Brave Heart's shoulder as he shook his hand with his right.

"Go now Mongoose Walking Proud and claim your victory," said Brave Heart with pride as he handed Mon-G Red Moons spear.

Mon-G's trek top the top of Mt. Rushmore was arduous. He had reached the peak just before sunset. The sun had set already for those below, but for Mon-G and the flock of geese flying overhead, it was still glowing red with streaks of gold offsetting it. Mongoose Walking Proud watched in awe at its decent over the horizon. A full moon had replaced the light lost as Mon-G painstakingly found his way back to the Ranger Station where Brave Heart was patiently awaiting.

Brave Heart couldn't help but think of the 10 Commandments legend as he witnessed Mongoose Walking Proud descending from the mountain with what looked like Mountain Lion skin wrapped around his broad shoulders and a Spear in hand held high with pride. Brave Heart was not surprised as he had come to think of Mon-g as a modern day Moses and knew he would return with a Spear. He had recognized it as once belonging to Running Bear. Upon closer inspection Brave Heart had realized that it was the very same Spear he had put up there earlier during winter. *It will be a great story to hear some new sun.*

Brave Heart and Mon-G had returned just before Dawn as Red Moon inspected the Spear and then handed it to Running Bear. Brave Heart walked up to Red Moon and put his hand on his shoulder.

"He is The One," said Brave Heart to Red Moon.

"Yes, he **is** The One," said Red Moon to Brave Heart as they turned to Running Bear.

"He is The One," said Red Moon and Brave Heart in unison to Chief Running Bear.

"He is The One!" announced Chief Running Bear, Brave Heart and Chief Red Moon in unison to the Cheyenne and Sioux Tribe as they began to rejoice in song and dance.

Mon-G walked to Fawn and collapsed in her arms as she rocked him.

"You are The One, son. You are The One," said Fawn with tremendous love and pride in her heartfelt words. Mon-G felt much comfort in Fawn's voice as he felt finally at peace.

"That's nice. That iisss niicce . . ." Darryl drifted away like a lonely boat on a vast ocean.

CHAPTER 17

The Homecoming

Dawn's parenTs haD never ventured to California and were in culture shock as Darryl drove them back to USC to meet up with Dawn and his parents. When they arrived at the front gate to the USC campus, Dawn and Darryl's family had already arrived. Darryl couldn't get out of the car fast enough, as Dawn had recognized her father's jeep and was in full sprint towards them.

"It's Dawn and my family!" Whelped Darryl as he sprinted towards Dawn as well.

They stood there in the middle of traffic in a strangling death lock daring anyone to deny them this moment. Dawn stopped kissing Darryl just long enough to whisper, "I love you Mongoose Walking Proud."

"I love you more, Dawn White Cloud," responded Mon-G as he kissed and embraced her as she did him.

"Okay you two let's get yall out the street," said Charles as he pushed them to the curb still entwined profusely within each other arms as they were oblivious to the horns yowling at them.

"I guess we have to introduce ourselves," said Charles as he shook Red Moon's hand.

Dawn and Darryl were unconscious of their families greeting one another in such a manner it would have made them both proud. Black Wolf had given his most cherished and beautifully decorated hatchet to Earl. Earl had passed on to Black Wolf a portable CD player and a collection of rap CD's of his favorite artists. Red Moon had presented Charles with his most cherished pipe and a pouch of his special blend of herbs. Red Moon, unwrapping his gift from Charles, was startled by the sudden screech of car tires. He turned around toward the sound and had seen a car speeding towards them. He dismissed it as some young man showing out his new car. Suddenly, an ear deafening shot rang out like a car backfiring. The screams that followed proved to him what he had feared.

"My God, she's shot!" Cried out Darryl to the top of his voice so terrified that it cracked.

Earl, very familiar with shootings, immediately accessed the situation as everyone else had their heads down or were running for cover. He had heard a revving of an engine soon after the shot and knew someone was the victim of a drive-by. He was surprised to see Black wolf standing his ground as well. From the layout of the school he knew he could get a look at the person as they came down the parallel road for it would have been the only way back to the main street. Earl took off through the campus to come up on the road leading back out to the main drag. Black wolf had instinctively followed behind him making sure to pick up the hatchet Earl had dropped in the excitement of the moment. He could still hear the screams of people crying out for someone to call 911. He thought the Spirits testing him as they had tested Mon-G and he would not fail them either.

Earl emerged from the campus to the street just ahead of the car as it sped towards him. He had pulled out a 9mm gun he always kept on him as most young men did in South Central and pointed it at the figure inside the car. He was just about to pull off a round when he gave pause at the face he was now close enough to recognize. It was . . .

"Moniqya? Shit!" snapped Earl as he jumped out the way just in time and landed on the hood of another car. He immediately started shooting into the back of Moniqya's car. Moniqya had squat her head down as she heard the rear window shatter. Her view was spoiled and when she reached the intersection she had been hit by a truck in her left front side, which spun her around in a clockwise 360 motion. Dazed, but somewhat still coherent of her situation, she exited the car. Blood was dripping profusely from her mouth as she held her broken ribs. Earl had given her up for done, but much to his demise she wasn't, as she lifted the gun and shot him square in the crest of his chest before he could comprehend his fate.

"No!" screamed Black Wolf. He was in full stride as he swung back and let loose the mighty hatchet. Moniqya was caught by surprise and didn't have time to react as the hatchet found a home between her bosom, piercing her heart as the force of the blow reeled her back and into the driver's side door as it collapsed from the impact. She was dead before she and the car door collapsed to the ground with a metal crunching thud.

Black Moon gently picked up Earl and carried him to the others as he prayed to the spirits to guide Earl well on his journey for he would surely pass onto them this day.

When Black Wolf emerged on the other side he could hear an ambulance in the distance. But what he saw sent a horrible feeling down his spine and deep into the depths of his soul. Mon-G was on the ground holding Dawn and rocking her back and forth like a frail little doll. She was motionless and there was blood all around. Dawn's precious blood. The whole family was in a panicked state. So much so, they had not even noticed him standing there with Earl in his arms. Black Wolf let the limp body of what was to be his future brother-in-law wither through his exhausted arms as he placed him gently on the campus grass.

"Why Spirits; Why Lord; Jesus Why; Why now; Why her; Why not me?" Cried Darryl a.k.a. Mon-G a.k.a. Mongoose Walking Proud. Everyone looked on, but none could answer. No One Answered.

CHAPTER 18

The One

I rise to the heavens
Feeling the gentle spray
Of dew like droplets
Against my skin
As I pass blooming white
clouds On the rise,
Cleansing my body, My spirit,
My soul
Before I come to you.
Blinding light gives way
To terrible darkness.
Yet I am not afraid.
I feel I can find you
Even in such an undiscovered place
As an incomprehensible force
Draws me to you.
Time passes, I know,
But it seems to have no meaning
As I'm still drawn to you,

Oblivious of all,
Yet desiring to know all.
I am compelled to cling on
To something not there.
Dare I return?
For undone wants and desires
Of all that was left behind?
I twirl in a spiral cascade
At the senseless effort
Of reaching for something,
Anything,
Which in turn is nothing.
I come to my senses
And reach out for you. I flow faster now
As can be told By the sounds
Now whispering
In my inner mind,
As I let go all inhibitions. I feel you,
Your force,
Now pushing me, Pulling me,
Behind me, Before me,
All around me, Drinking me,
Swallowing me, Enveloping me.
I am cool,
Warm, Cold, Hot.
I am in immense pain
As I feel what you suffer.
I am in immeasurable ecstasy
As I feel your love.
So deep am I now into you, I am one,
We are one.
There are others,
So many countless others,
But it is only you I truly feel.
You are The One,
The First, The Last,

MANLY E. HOGG

The Beginning, The End,
The All
And I am cradled to you,
In bliss of your greatness,
Knowing all
As I receive the Gift of you. I am open,
So deeply open
To you and all.
Here I belong.
Here I will stay,
Knowing truth,
Knowing all,
Knowing you,
THE ONE.

CHAPTER 19

The Crossings

Darryl haD never witness such tranquility in reality as what he was gazing upon today on Oahe Lake. He could remember a place such as this when he was in his dream-state but there was something about **now** that made it different. To know a love such as he knew with Dawn had made all the difference in the world. "They couldn't have been in a better place during their crossings,

Chief," said Mon-G solemnly to Red Moon.

"I agree, young Mon-G," said Red Moon as he placed his hand on Mon-G's shoulder to comfort him.

Mon-G was dressed in traditional Cheyenne garbs with a Warrior's Bonnet and moccasin boots. Dawn's family were traditionally dressed as well. Darryl's mother and sister had worn black dresses and his father his best black suit.

The climate on the lake was somewhat cool for spring but that was normal considering the late winter South Dakota experienced during the earlier part of the year. Black Wolf put the final touches on the burial boats and motioned to his father that everything was in order.

"Mongoose Walking Proud of the Cheyenne Warrior Cast. Would you do me an honor and set our loved ones free so they may walk among the ancients in spirit form to continue guiding us through to a proud and honorable existence?" asked Chief Red Moon of Mon-G as he handed him a burning torch.

Mon-G nervously retrieved the torch from Red Moon and walked to the edge of the lakebed. He couldn't help but thank the spirits that his father allowed him to hold a funeral for his brother in this manner. Charles always wanted to be cremated himself so he didn't see where this way would make much a difference. If anything it was more natural and compassionate he had thought than using a furnace.

Mon-G lit the two boats as the bodies inside them were covered with a mound of wood branches. He pushed one away from the bank as Black Wolf pushed the other.

"It is done," said Mon-G solemnly to all that watched as the boats burst into towering infernos. Ancient Chants and drumming began as if to wake up the Spirits for the arrival of two newly freed souls.

Mon-G walked over to a figure sitting in a wheelchair and placed his hands on their shoulders as he bent over to kiss the sweet lips of his Dawns'.

"I'm very sorry about your grandfathers untimely demise. Thank you for allowing us to bury...ah, sendoff Earl as well. I think he would have liked to go this way," said Darryl solemnly as tears rolled down his cheeks. Dawn was crying too and she held Darryl's head close to her with her left hand as her right arm was immobilized with a shoulder cast for a broken collarbone she suffered when the bullet impacted.

"I love you so much Darryl," cried Dawn.

"I love you more, baby. You are The One. You will always be The One," answered Mon-G as he walked around to face Dawn.

"This may not be the right time but the Spirits are moving me," said Darryl as he fell to one knee.

"Dawn White Cloud will you do me the honor of marrying me? "Yes, Mongoose Walking Proud, I would be honored for you are The One."

EPILOGUE

"Ouch, baby waTch it!" Whelped Darryl as Dawn painstakingly pulled another hair from one of the many ingrown hair bumps peppered along his delicately skinned face.

"Ah... don't be such a baby, you should be used to it by now," said Dawn trying not to giggle at the concerned expression on Darryl's handsome face.

"I sure hope you don't perform surgery the way you pick my face," said Darryl jokingly.

"Well, I sure hope you're not so sensitive when your NFL playmates tackle you," said Dawn as she mounted her husband.

"I got your sensitive right here," said Darryl as he pulled Dawn into him and kissed her sweet tender lips.

"Hmmm... I love you Mongoose Walking Proud." "I love you more, Mrs. Dawn Jackson."

"Mommy, Daddy, Earl won't let me watch Teletubbies," said Jewel as she jumped up on the bed.

"I want to watch Barney, Mommy," said Earl as he followed suit. "Why you on Daddy, Mommy?" asked Jewel as her 4 year old mind strained to know all.

"Me and your Dad are just wrestling dear."

"I want to wrestle too, Daddy," said Earl as his 5 year old mind was always looking for something fun to do even if it meant tormenting his sister in the process.

"Come here you two," said Mon-G as he playfully wrestled with his children.

Dawn looked on with amazement at her family. She felt truly blessed by the spirits. A heartfelt tear of pride and joy found its way from the depths of her soul to the corner of her eye as it dripped freely to the plush carpet floor.

"Okay, tag me Jewel," cried out Dawn as she flopped on top of Darryl to attempt to pull her lovely daughter free from his onslaught of tickles.

Earl commenced to count his sister out as he slapped the bed in unison,

"One…two…three…you lose and Daddy and I wins…yeah!"

"Oh yeah, KD called earlier, something about her trying to get her son back. I guess she needs our help."

Dawn collapsed on the bed as if a great weight suddenly came upon her. Her tone became solemn. "I knew this day would come, it was why she became a lawyer."

"Didn't she get the partnership with her Law firm?"

"Yes, but I knew even such a tremendous achievement would still leave a void in her life…but for now let's just chill for a moment."

Dawn and Darryl embraced one another and then their children. There, they laid sprawled listlessly on the king-sized bed of their 10-bedroom mansion, which overlooked a wondrous lake, in South Dakota exhausted from laughter, as they lived on, content and happily, evermore.

www.ingramcontent.com/pod-product-compliance
Ingram Content Group UK Ltd.
Pitfield, Milton Keynes, MK11 3LW, UK
UKHW022221230426
12048UKWH00016BA/990